'Are you pregnant, Zoë?'

The question caught her off-guard. Her eyes flew to his face, but it was impossible to tell what he was thinking. He was deliberately masking his feelings, and the thought made her shiver—because the Ben she remembered would never have been so guarded around her; she would have known immediately how he was feeling.

She half rose, but Ben was too quick for her. He caught her hand. 'I'm not letting you run away without answering my question. You're having my baby, aren't you, Zoë? Why else would you have come here to see me?'

Raising her head, she looked him in the eyes. 'Yes, I'm pregnant.'

After a momentary pause, Ben gave her one of his trademark grins. 'I may be shocked to learn that I'm about to become a father, but I'm pleased too. I've never made any secret of the fact that I want kids—although I rather hoped I'd have a wife before they came along…'

Dear Reader

I always knew that the third book in my *Dalverston Weddings* series would be the most difficult to write. Not only did I feel a very special bond with Ben and Zoë, so wanted to do them justice, but I was aware that I was going to give them an extremely tough time.

When best man Ben Nicholls discovers that his ex-girlfriend Zoë Frost is to attend the wedding, he is stunned. He has spent the past two years trying to forget about her, yet as soon as he sees her again all the old feelings resurface. When Zoë agrees to spend one last night with him, Ben is certain that it will help him to draw a line under the past.

When Zoë tells Ben a few months later that he is to be a father, he is both shocked and elated. However, it isn't the only thing that Zoë needs to tell him. There is something else—something that rocks his world. All Ben knows is that he intends to be there for Zoë and their baby, no matter what happens.

Helping Ben and Zoë deal with such life-changing issues was a challenge. I cried with them during the tough times and laughed with them during the good—it was a real emotional roller coaster. I hope you enjoy this book, and that you will feel at the end of it, as I did, that this couple truly deserve a lifetime of happiness together.

Best wishes

Jennifer

THE DOCTOR'S BABY BOMBSHELL

BY
JENNIFER TAYLOR

MILLS & BOON®
Pure reading pleasure™

DID YOU PURCHASE THIS BOOK WITHOUT A COVER?

If you did, you should be aware it is **stolen property** as it was reported *unsold and destroyed* by a retailer. Neither the author nor the publisher has received any payment for this book.

All the characters in this book have no existence outside the imagination of the author, and have no relation whatsoever to anyone bearing the same name or names. They are not even distantly inspired by any individual known or unknown to the author, and all the incidents are pure invention.

All Rights Reserved including the right of reproduction in whole or in part in any form. This edition is published by arrangement with Harlequin Enterprises II BV/S.à.r.l. The text of this publication or any part thereof may not be reproduced or transmitted in any form or by any means, electronic or mechanical, including photocopying, recording, storage in an information retrieval system, or otherwise, without the written permission of the publisher.

This book is sold subject to the condition that it shall not, by way of trade or otherwise, be lent, resold, hired out or otherwise circulated without the prior consent of the publisher in any form of binding or cover other than that in which it is published and without a similar condition including this condition being imposed on the subsequent purchaser.

® and TM are trademarks owned and used by the trademark owner and/or its licensee. Trademarks marked with ® are registered with the United Kingdom Patent Office and/or the Office for Harmonisation in the Internal Market and in other countries.

First published in Great Britain 2009
Harlequin Mills & Boon Limited,
Eton House, 18-24 Paradise Road, Richmond, Surrey TW9 1SR

© Jennifer Taylor 2009

ISBN: 978 0 263 86831 9

Set in Times Roman 10¼ on 12¾ pt
03-0309-54895

Printed and bound in Spain
by Litografia Rosés, S.A., Barcelona

Jennifer Taylor lives in the north-west of England, in a small village surrounded by some really beautiful countryside. She has written for several different Mills & Boon® series in the past, but it wasn't until she read her first Medical™ Romance that she truly found her niche. She was so captivated by these heart-warming stories that she set out to write them herself!

When she's not writing, or doing research for her latest book, Jennifer's hobbies include reading, gardening, travel, and chatting to friends both on and off-line. She is always delighted to hear from readers, so do visit her website at www.jennifer-taylor.com

Recent titles by the same author:

THE GP'S MEANT-TO-BE BRIDE*
MARRYING THE RUNAWAY BRIDE*
THE SURGEON'S FATHERHOOD SURPRISE**
THEIR LITTLE CHRISTMAS MIRACLE

*Dalverston Weddings
**Brides of Penhally Bay

For The Wedding Party: Vicky and Jamie,
Kathy, Carl, Pauline, John, Nigel, Neil, Mark, Mel.
And last but never least, Bill.
Thank you all for an unforgettable day.

CHAPTER ONE

December

SHE shouldn't have come. It was all very well thinking that she was ready to face Ben while there were hundreds of miles separating them, but now that she was here, she was no longer as confident. Could she really see Ben again, talk to him, and not allow her resolve to weaken?

Zoë Frost could feel her stomach churning with nerves as the taxi drew up outside the hotel. When she had received the invitation to Ross and Heather's wedding, she had dismissed the idea of attending. After all, when she had left Dalverston two years ago, she had sworn she would never go back. Nevertheless, as the weeks had passed, bringing the day ever closer, she had felt increasingly torn.

There were very few people to whom she was close. It had been her decision not to form attachments, neither romantic ones nor those of friendship. In her experience people invariably let you down and it was easier to keep your distance. However, Ross and Heather had proved themselves to be true friends. They had always been there for her and had never taken offence when she had brushed them off, as she'd so frequently done in the past. How could she not attend their wedding given those facts? Maybe it would be hard to see Ben again, but she owed it to them to be there when they got married.

'This is your hotel, miss.'

Zoë jumped when the taxi driver reminded her that he was waiting for her to alight. Hunting in her black leather bag, she drew out her purse and paid him, fumbling a little as she added a generous tip to the fare. She'd been living in Paris for the past two years and her brain hadn't caught up with the change of currency on the short flight back to England.

A porter came out of the hotel to collect her luggage and she tipped him as well, smiling wryly as she realised how used she'd grown to dealing with such matters. The time she'd spent in Paris had changed her, smoothed away the rough edges. On the outside at least she was no longer the gauche, inexperienced girl from the care home, but a woman who had learned how to blend in with the highest levels of society. The thought was a welcome boost to her confidence.

Zoë checked in and went upstairs to her room. It was a beautiful room but then she had made a point of booking one with a view over the countryside. Although she loved Paris, she had missed all this, missed the space, the light, the majesty of the hills that towered over the town. Opening the window, she breathed deeply, letting the cold December air flow into her lungs. Coming back to Dalverston was like coming home, she thought, then quickly dismissed the idea. It was too dangerous to think like that, too emotive, and if there was one thing she needed more than anything today it was to keep control of her emotions. She wouldn't be able to cope when she saw Ben if she didn't.

Once again Zoë felt the stirring of doubt but she brushed it aside. Opening her case, she took out the chic honey-gold wool suit she had chosen to wear for the occasion. There was an ivory silk blouse to go with it plus a pair of wickedly high-heeled shoes that added several inches to her not-inconsiderable height. The outfit had cost a small fortune but it would be worth it if it helped her project the right image, that of a woman in control. How she felt inside was her business. She didn't intend to let anyone know how nervous she felt. She shot a glance at the clock on the bedside table and felt her heart surge. In just under an hour's time she would see Ben.

Ben parked his car in the hotel's car park. Opening the door of the sleek little convertible, he eased his legs out from under the wheel, sighing when he saw the mud that was caked on the knees of his jeans. He really should have changed before he'd come here. Normally, he would have done so, but he wasn't firing on all cylinders today and was it any wonder?

When he'd seen Zoë's name on that guest list Ross had given him that morning, he'd had the devil of a job hiding his shock. He had never expected her to attend the wedding even though he knew that Heather and Ross were her closest friends. He had assumed that she would make some excuse, but obviously not. Why *had* she decided to come? he wondered. Was it just because she wanted to see her friends get married or was there another reason, one that had something to do with him?

Ben swore under his breath as he made his way into the hotel. Zoë had made her feelings perfectly clear two years ago and it was madness to imagine that she'd changed her mind. He wouldn't want her to either. He'd learned a valuable lesson when she'd left him and he had no intention of placing himself in the position of having his heart trampled on a second time. Maybe he had believed in love once upon a time but he didn't believe in it now. Zoë had cured him of that kind of misty-eyed thinking!

Walking over to the reception desk, Ben joined the queue

and waited his turn to speak to the receptionist. There were a lot of people milling about and he guessed that most of them were wedding guests too. He sighed. A lot of folk were going to be upset by what had happened.

The lift bell pinged as the lift arrived at the ground floor and Ben automatically glanced round, then felt his breath catch when he saw the woman who alighted. Tall and slender, with her red-gold hair pulled smoothly back from her face, she drew many admiring glances. Ben knew that he was staring at her, but he couldn't help it. She looked exactly the same in many ways and yet so very different in others.

He took rapid stock, trying to work out what had changed. There was no doubt that the honey-coloured suit she was wearing was expensive. The cut of the fabric hinted at expert tailoring of a type rarely seen in chain-store clothing. Her shoes—the sexiest pair of shoes he had ever seen with those wickedly high heels—also betrayed their pedigree, as did the matching bag that swung from her hand. She looked so cool, so poised, so *sophisticated* that Ben felt pain stab through his heart. Obviously, Zoë had lost no time encasing herself in yet another protective layer.

She was halfway across the foyer when she spotted him. Ben took a deep breath when he saw her stop and got a grip of himself. He had come here to break the news to her and the sooner he got it over with, the better. Stepping out of the queue, he headed towards her, fixing his most urbane smile into place as he drew closer. He may have loved Zoë once but that was all in the past. Their relationship was history now and he'd moved on…

Hadn't he?

Ben clamped down on that thought as he greeted her. 'Hello, Zoë. How are you? Although I doubt if I need to ask that when you're looking so stunning.'

His tone was playful, the one he used whenever he was around any attractive woman. Most seemed to enjoy the hint of flirtatiousness in his voice, the suggestion that there might be something more to come, although Zoë obviously didn't appreciate it.

'I'm very well, thank you, Ben. How are you?'

Her deep grey eyes looked dispassionately back at him but Ben held his smile, determined not to let her see how discomfited he felt. 'Great. Or as great as I can be in the circumstances.'

'That sounds very cryptic.' One elegant brow arched as she looked at him and Ben sighed. He was here to deliver a message, not to pander to his ego by playing silly games.

'I didn't intend it to. Sorry. I'm afraid I have some rather bad news, Zoë.' Glancing around, he spotted a couple of chairs in an alcove by the window and nodded towards them. 'Let's sit down over there, shall we?'

Zoë looked sharply at him but she didn't demur. Walking over to the chairs, she sat down, smoothing her skirt over her knees. Ben caught a tantalising glimpse of her elegant legs encased in whisper-fine stockings and hastily averted his eyes. Zoë had always hated going out with bare legs—she preferred to wear stockings instead. He'd watched her put them on many times and enjoyed the experience too.

He gritted his teeth as an image of her drawing the fine silk over her shapely calves flashed into his head. This was dangerous territory and he refused to go there, especially today.

'What's this all about, Ben? What sort of bad news do you have to tell me?'

Her tone was sharp; it cut through his thoughts and helped him focus. Leaning forward, he fixed her with a level look. 'The wedding has been called off.'

'Called off?' She stared at him in disbelief. 'If this is a joke, Ben, I really don't appreciate it.'

She went to rise but he caught hold of her hand and stopped her. 'It isn't a joke, Zoë. I wouldn't joke about something like this.'

She had the grace to look momentarily uncomfortable before she rallied. Sinking back down onto the chair, she eased her hand out of his grasp. 'I apologise. So tell me what's happened.'

Ben shrugged, needing a little more time to regain his own composure. The feel of her slender fingers had released a whole raft of emotions he hadn't been prepared for. If he'd moved on, as he'd thought, why was his heart thumping as though it was trying to leap out of his chest? He'd held her hand, for heaven's sake, not made mad, passionate love to her!

'Heather called it off,' he explained, closing his mind to any more foolish ideas of that nature. He refused to torment himself by recalling how good it had been when he and Zoë had made love. 'She told Ross that she'd decided it would be a mistake if they got married.'

'A mistake?' Zoë's brow wrinkled. 'But they're perfect for each other. Anyone can see that.'

'Well, apparently, *anyone* would be wrong.' Ben sighed when he saw her face close up. 'I don't mean to sound facetious but I was as stunned as you are when Ross told me. In fact, I'm still trying to take it in. I was all geared up to do my best man bit when I woke up this morning, but it seems my services won't be needed after all.'

'Is that why you're dressed like that?' Zoë glanced down at his jeans, her nose wrinkling in distaste as she took stock of the crust of mud that adorned them, and he chuckled.

'It wasn't a deliberate choice because I was peeved about not getting to read my speech, if that's what you're thinking.'

A tiny smile twitched the corners of her beautiful mouth. 'I'm glad to hear it. It would seem a little extreme.'

Her eyes rose to his and his breath caught when he saw the

warmth they held. It had been so long since Zoë had looked at him this way. In the last painful weeks of their relationship all they'd done was argue. There'd been no warmth then, no fun, no closeness, just a determination on both sides to get their own way. All of a sudden Ben regretted how he'd behaved, regretted pushing her to accept how he'd felt. No wonder she had run away when he'd put her under so much pressure. Maybe he had loved her desperately but he should have tried to win her round in a different way.

Regrets tumbled around inside his head but it was too late for them now. At least he and Zoë were on speaking terms and that was something. 'I ended up getting called out to an incident at the canal,' he explained, hoping to solder their fragile truce. If there was one thing that Zoë truly cared about it was work—his job, her job, anything to do with medicine. 'In fact, Ross went along as well, and the rest of the guys from the surgery. That accounts for my current less than sartorial look. It was *extremely* mucky down there.'

'Good heavens!' Zoë leant forward and he could see the interest in her eyes. 'It must have been a major incident if Ambulance Control drafted in so many extra people.'

'It was, although normally the rapid response unit would have had it covered,' he explained, responding to her enthusiasm. One of the best things about their relationship had been the fact that they'd shared a love of emergency medicine. They'd spent a lot of their time discussing the cases they'd seen, although now that he thought about it, Ben wondered if it was normal for a couple to spend so much time talking about work. Had it been a way to paper over the cracks in their relationship, perhaps?

'Why weren't they able to deal with it today?' Zoë asked curiously.

Ben pushed the thought aside. In truth, it shouldn't have bothered him and the fact that it did had him hurrying on. 'Most of the emergency response vehicles are out of commission at the moment. There's a problem with the fuel supply, apparently. That's why the surgery was contacted, and how Ross and I ended up helping out. It certainly wasn't what we had planned for today.'

'No, of course not.' Zoë sighed. 'Poor Ross, he must be devastated. And Heather too. She couldn't have taken such a decision lightly.'

'I don't imagine so,' Ben concurred, wondering if he should explain that Ross hadn't appeared to be that cut up about what had happened. In the end, he decided not to say anything. People responded differently and who was he to judge?

'What's happening about the guests?' Zoë frowned as she looked around the foyer. 'I expect a lot of them are staying here. Do they all know that the wedding has been called off?'

'I did my best to let everyone know, but I wasn't all that successful, unfortunately.' He saw the question in her eyes and continued. 'Ross gave me the guest list and asked if I'd do the honours. I got in touch with as many people as I could, but some had already left home by the time I phoned. Ross has arranged for the vicar to meet any who slipped through the net when they turn up at the church.'

'What a mess!' Zoë exclaimed. 'It's going to cause a real stir, isn't it? I'd hate to be in Ross's or Heather's shoes for the next few weeks.'

'It won't hit Heather as hard. She's gone to London—caught the train last night, I believe. At least she'll be spared a lot of the flak.'

'I see.' Zoë gave a little sigh and then stood up. 'Well, thanks for letting me know what's happened, Ben. It's a real shame, but if it wasn't going to work, it's probably best that Heather called things off.'

'I'm sure you're right,' Ben agreed, feeling something akin to panic grip him. Was that it? Was Zoë going to bid him goodbye and leave? There was nothing to keep her here now, nothing and no one.

That thought stung more than it should have done and it annoyed him too. He was over Zoë and he refused to let her influence his life in any way, shape or form. He stood up as well, a polite little smile curving his mouth, a smile that was guaranteed to convince her that he was well and truly over her. 'When are you flying back to Paris?'

'Tomorrow lunchtime.' She glanced at her watch and grimaced. 'I've got hours to kill now, unless I can re-book onto an earlier flight.'

'Sounds like a lot of hassle to me,' he said lightly. 'Why don't you stick to your original plan and enjoy a day here instead?'

'Doing what?' She glanced down at the elegant suit that clung to every delicious curve of her body. 'I didn't exactly come equipped for a weekend in the country.'

'I could lend you some stuff.' He managed a couldn't-careless smile when she looked at him, although he was as surprised as she was that he'd made the suggestion. 'All you need is a pair of jeans, a sweater and a jacket,' he continued because there was no way he could stop now he'd begun. 'And you're ready for anything.'

'Such as what?' she demanded with a touch of challenge in her voice.

'Oh, I don't know…how about a hike up into the hills to get some fresh air?'

He glanced out of the window, using the moment to gather his thoughts. He hadn't planned on spending any time with Zoë while she was here, but wouldn't it prove, once and for all, that he was over her? Ever since he'd seen her name on that guest list he'd felt uneasy and he hated feeling that he wasn't in control. Zoë had hurt him badly, destroyed his faith in love and commitment, all the givens he'd once believed in. He may appear the same old Ben on the outside, always up for some fun and ready to enjoy a joke, but inside he was a completely different person.

He no longer believed that love could conquer any obstacle. He no longer believed that two people were meant to be together. When Zoë had left him, turned her back on him and his love, she had destroyed all those certainties he had taken for granted. He would never love anyone the way he had loved Zoë. He would never allow himself to love that deeply again.

'It is a gorgeous day,' she said wistfully, and he glanced back at her.

'Is that a yes, then?'

'I don't know.' Her gaze lifted to his and he saw her mentally raise the barriers. 'I didn't plan on spending any time with you, Ben.'

'I'm sure you didn't.' He ignored the jibe, didn't even flinch when the arrow pierced his skin. He knew how she felt, that she didn't want him and never would. Zoë didn't *do* commitment. She didn't do love and marriage and happy-ever-after, and he had accepted that. However, this time with her could be just what he needed to lay the past to rest.

'I didn't plan on spending time with you either, Zoë, but neither of us could have foretold what was going to happen. Why don't we make the best of a bad job?'

His tone was calm and it seemed to work. He saw her relax and carried on, inwardly smiling. He had women falling at his feet, women eager to spend days—and nights!—with him but he didn't want any of them at the moment. He wanted these few hours with Zoë to prove he could cope without her.

'We're both at a loose end this afternoon and we can fill in the time by having a walk, maybe even have dinner later if we're not too knackered by then.' He shrugged, a gesture that reeked of indifference even though he wanted this very much. 'At least the weekend won't have been a complete loss, will it? So what do you say, Zoë? It's up to you.'

CHAPTER TWO

THEY drove to Capper's Fell and parked in a lay-by. Zoë got out of the car, trying not to think about the last time they'd been there. There was no point looking back when she wouldn't have done things any differently. She didn't want to get married, didn't want children, didn't want to spend her life with Ben or anyone else. She had seen the damage love could do, suffered because of it, and she didn't intend to give anyone that much power over her.

'I thought we could walk to the top and down the far side if you're up to it,' Ben announced as he joined her and she nodded.

'Fine by me.'

'Sure you can manage in those boots? They are a little on the large side for you.'

He crouched down and began tugging at the laces of her borrowed boots. One of his sisters had left them at his house, he'd explained, and although they were half a size too big, Zoë had assured him they would be fine. Now she found herself wishing that she'd told him they had fitted perfectly. At least then she wouldn't have had to suffer in silence as his fingers gently prodded her toes.

Heat flashed along her veins and she shifted her feet, wanting to make him stop. She could cope so long as Ben didn't touch her, didn't make her remember all the other occasions when his hands had caressed her. He'd been such a passionate lover, showing her with his hands and his mouth how much he had wanted her. Zoë had tried to hold something of herself back, to not respond so fully, so completely, but she'd never succeeded. When Ben had made love to her, she had given him everything—her heart, her mind and her soul. And that's what had scared her most of all. She had no control when she was in Ben's arms.

'They're perfectly adequate for the amount of walking we're going to be doing today,' she said briskly, moving away.

'Good.'

He didn't react to her brusqueness as he straightened and contrarily Zoë wished he had done so. At least she would have had an outlet for her feelings if they'd had one of their rows.

She sighed as she followed him to the stile. Was that what she really wanted, to fight with him like she'd done in the last weeks they'd been together? Every day had been a battle, every minute they'd spent together so full of tension that she'd felt sick all the time. Ben had wanted her to give in and accept that they could be happy together for ever and ever, but she'd known it wouldn't work.

Love might seem endless in the beginning but it didn't last. Once passion faded, interest waned, and that was when the problems began. Even though she'd been only ten when her parents had divorced, she'd endured years of anguish beforehand as she'd watched her mother and father tearing themselves and each other apart.

It had been a relief when she'd been taken into care after her mother had suffered a breakdown following the divorce. By that time her father had left England and made a new life for himself in Australia; he hadn't wanted the responsibility of caring for a ten-year-old child. The social workers had tried to explain it to her as gently as possible but Zoë had understood: her father didn't want her.

Life in the children's home had been bleak but at least there'd been nobody there she had cared about, and nobody who had cared about her either. She'd been freed from the emotional trauma of watching the people she loved destroy their lives. Her mother had never fully recovered from her breakdown and had been deemed too fragile to take care of her so Zoë had stayed in the home until she was sixteen when she had moved into a hostel. They exchanged Christmas and birthday cards but that was all. Their relationship had ended a long time ago.

'Careful! It's very slippery on this side. Here, take my hand.'

Ben grasped her hand as she climbed over the first bit of the stile and Zoë managed not to pull away, but her reluctance to let him help her must have shown. His mouth thinned but once again he didn't say anything and it surprised her. Was Ben afraid of causing a row? she wondered. He must be as aware as she was of how fragile their truce really was.

The thought helped her put everything into perspective. Zoë realised that she had to do her bit to make the day as stress-free as possible for both of them. She nodded her thanks as she alighted from the stile, feeling her heart catch when Ben smiled at her. He had always worn his heart on his sleeve in the past where she'd been concerned. He'd never been able to hide how much he had loved her and it had made her own reserve all the more marked. However, she'd been afraid to lower her guard, apart from when they had made love.

How did he feel about her now? Although his smile seemed genuine enough, it was impossible to tell what he was thinking, and it troubled her. The old Ben had been so open about his feelings and she hated to think that he had changed so much. She might not be capable of giving herself to him but it didn't mean she didn't care about him.

They were halfway up the hill when Ben suddenly stopped. Zoë just managed to stop as well before she cannoned into him. She frowned when she saw him turn and look over to their left.

'What's wrong?'

'I thought I heard something—a moan or a shout, I'm not sure.'

He shrugged, his handsome face looking unusually stern as he stared across the open countryside. Zoë realised with a start how much older he looked than the last time she'd seen him. There were lines around his hazel eyes that definitely hadn't been there two years ago and silver threads laced through his dark brown hair. Even the contours of his face had changed. He'd always been an extremely handsome man, and he still was, but there was a new austerity about his features, an authority that merely added to his appeal. At thirty-four years of age, Ben was in his prime and he looked it too.

A shiver ran down her spine as her brain logged all the small but significant changes. It was an effort to focus on the present but she couldn't afford not to. There was no future for her and Ben—there never had been.

'Do you think someone's in trouble?' she asked, deliberately removing any trace of emotion from her voice.

'It could have been a bird, I suppose…'

'But you don't think so?' she finished for him and he sighed.

'No. I'm ninety per cent certain that I heard someone calling and that it came from over there.'

'So what do you want to do?'

'I don't think we have much choice. We'll have to take a look.'

Zoë followed as he turned off the main path. They had to

walk in single file because the track was so narrow. It was lined on both sides with prickly bushes which snagged their trousers as they forced a way through them.

'This must be a sheep track,' Ben called over his shoulder.

'Pity the poor sheep if they have to wriggle through all these thorns,' Zoë retorted, and he chuckled.

'I imagine it's a bit different to strolling down the Champs Elysées.'

'It certainly is. You might get jostled about on the pavement there but you definitely don't have to pick thorns out of your flesh when you get home,' she replied, and he laughed again, a rich deep sound that made her skin tingle.

It took them a good five minutes to reach the spot Ben had pointed out but there was nobody in sight. He sighed as he stared around. 'Looks like I've brought you on a wild-goose chase. Sorry.'

'It doesn't matter,' she began then broke off when she heard a low moan. 'There is someone here!' she exclaimed, trying to locate from where the sound had come. It came again and she pointed towards a huge spiky bush off to their right. 'There!'

Ben hurried forwards, the wicked-looking thorns tearing at his hands as he parted the branches. 'It's a child! I'll see if I can get her out.'

'Here, let me help you.'

Zoë forced her way through the undergrowth, wincing as the thorns dug into her. She could see the child now lying right in the very centre of the bush. Heaven only knew how she had got in there but that wasn't nearly as important as getting her out. Dragging the sleeves of the borrowed jacket over her hands to protect them, she pulled the branches apart until there was a big enough gap for Ben to reach in and lift the child out. He carried her to a clearing and laid her on the ground then stripped off his jacket and covered her with it. Zoë knelt down and checked her pulse.

'Pulse is slow but at least there is one.' She laid her hand on the child's forehead and grimaced. 'She's very cold. I don't know how long she's been out here but it looks like hypothermia to me.'

'We need to get her to hospital.' Ben looked back the way they had come. 'The quickest way is to carry her back to the car and drive her there. We can't afford to wait around for an ambulance in view of the problems they're having at the moment. We'll check her over first just to be on the safe side, but we don't want to delay too long.'

They worked together, performing a rapid but thorough examination. Zoë would have liked some basic equipment to work with but as it wasn't available, she got on with the job as best she could. She rattled out her findings as she went so that Ben could check they hadn't missed anything.

'Skin is very pale and her face looks puffy. Breathing is slow and quite shallow, too.'

Ben had slid his hand under the child's sweater and was feeling her armpit. 'Very cold under the arms so hypothermia is fairly advanced.' He tested the little girl's limbs next. 'No sign of fractures—can you check her spine?'

'That seems fine,' Zoë told him a moment later.

'Good. It should be safe enough to move her.' He felt in his jacket pocket and pulled out a woollen hat which he placed on the child's head to help conserve any remaining body heat. 'That's the best we can do for now. Let's get her to hospital.'

He picked up the child and headed back along the track. Zoë followed him, wishing there was something she could do to help. It wasn't easy forging a way through the bushes when he was so hampered but it was impossible to walk alongside him and assist in any way.

'This is so frustrating,' she grumbled as she trotted along at his heels. 'I should be helping you instead of acting like a spare part!'

'Your turn will come,' he told her and even though she couldn't see his face, she could hear the smile in his voice.

'Why do I get the feeling that my turn might not be all that pleasant?' she demanded. 'Exactly what do you have in mind?'

'Ah, that would be telling. And there is no way that I want to scare you off. I need you, Zoë Frost, and I don't intend to let you get away from me!'

Ben grimaced, hoping Zoë wouldn't take his comment the wrong way. He breathed a sigh of relief when she laughed. He really mustn't go looking for hidden meanings, he told himself as they rejoined the main path, and definitely not allow himself to wonder if Zoë was looking for them too. Zoë wasn't his girl-friend any longer. She wasn't going to be a part of his life either. Once today was over, he probably wouldn't see her again.

The thought caused a funny sensation in the pit of his stomach but Ben ignored it. They had reached the stile and he waited while Zoë scrambled over to the other side then passed the child across to her.

'It's OK, I've got her,' she told him when he went to take the little girl back and he nodded. It didn't matter to him if she preferred to struggle rather than accept his help. He knew how independent she was and if it made her feel better, who was he to object?

Unlocking the car, he hunkered down and slid the driver's seat forward as far as it would go. There was a tiny bench seat in the back—so small that he used it merely to stow his coat. However, it would be needed for a different purpose today. 'Can you climb into the back? I know it's going to be a tight squeeze but I want to lay her on the front seat. I can lower the back to make it more comfortable for her if you could hunch up.'

Zoë shot a wry glance into the back of the car. 'So this is what you meant about my turn. I'm going to have to perform some contortions, am I?'

Ben grinned. 'It's either you or me, and I honestly don't think I can get in there. I'd need a shoehorn to fit into that minuscule space!'

'Either that or a bucket of grease,' she retorted, handing him the child before doubling up and scrambling into the back of the car. Ben had a tantalising glimpse of her shapely bottom then she was in, wriggling herself into the corner to allow for the passenger seat to be reclined.

He drove the enticing image from his head as he gently laid the little girl on the passenger seat and adjusted the back until she was lying almost flat. He fastened the seat belt across her then handed Zoë his mobile phone.

'Can you call the emergency services and tell them what's happened? No doubt there's some frantic parents looking for this little one and the sooner they know she's been found, the better.' He closed the door and strode round to the driver's side, grunting as he squeezed behind the steering-wheel. 'I only hope I can change gear with my knees tucked under my chin.'

'We can always trade places,' Zoë suggested sweetly and he chuckled.

'No way! I could do myself permanent damage if I got in there.'

He pulled out of the lay-by, leaving Zoë to inform everyone about what had happened. He could hear her talking on the phone, her voice sounding cool and crisp as she relayed the in-formation. She had a lot more confidence than she'd had two years ago, he realised. Although she'd always been very self-assured in her dealings with her patients, she'd been more reticent when it had come to speaking to people in authority. Obviously, the time she'd spent in Paris had brought about changes in her attitude as well as in her appearance and Ben couldn't help wondering if it was all down to Zoë herself or to other forces.

Had Zoë met someone there, a man who had shown her how to dress to make the most of herself, taught her to feel as confident as she was beautiful? The idea didn't sit easily with him even though it had nothing to do with him if it turned out to be true. Zoë didn't need him as her mentor or her lover.

The child's name was Megan Turner. She was four years old and had been visiting her grandparents who had a farm in the area when she had wandered off. Her parents met them at the hospital, overjoyed that she had been found. Ben explained his suspicions that Megan was suffering from hypothermia but he didn't waste time. It was more important that Megan receive the appropriate treatment.

'I don't think she's bad enough to warrant controlled warming but can you alert PICU just in case?' he instructed as he shouldered open the doors to Resus. He placed Megan on a bed then glanced at the two nurses and junior doctor who had followed him in. 'Can you take her temperature, Abby—use a rectal thermometer, please. I want to know exactly what we're dealing with. Jo, I want you to fill the bath with warm water and, Adam, I want you to monitor her breathing and pulse rate. Any fluctuation—and I do mean *any*—I want to be informed immediately.'

Everyone nodded and set to work. Zoë watched them, enjoying the way they all seemed to know exactly what was expected of them. It was typical of Ben to make his instructions crystal clear. He hated mistakes being made and did everything possible to avoid them. She'd learned such a lot from him when they had worked together…

And learned even more when they were away from work, a small voice whispered inside her head.

'Want to give me a hand?'

Zoë started when Ben turned to her, feeling the colour rush up her face as she prayed that he didn't have any inkling about what she'd been thinking. 'Of course. What do you want me to do?'

'Check her response to both noise and light.' He lowered his voice. 'She hasn't opened her eyes or spoken since we found her but I don't think she's unconscious, just exhausted and very frightened. I want to do the absolute minimum to guarantee her well-being rather than rush in with all guns blazing.'

Zoë nodded, understanding why he preferred that approach. Although the dramatic scenes that were the staple of so many medical soap operas made excellent viewing, a patient's needs were better served if treatment was kept as minimal as possible. She took a penlight out of its holder and gently peeled back the little girl's eyelids while she shone the light into her eyes. There was an immediate response and she glanced at Ben.

'Both eyes reacting positively to light.'

'Good.'

Ben's tone was abstracted as he bent over the child, but Zoë didn't doubt that he had taken her findings on board. She replaced the light in its holder and picked up a pair of plastic forceps which she rapped on the metal bedframe. Little Megan visibly jumped, confirming Ben's suspicions that she wasn't comatose. It was an encouraging finding and Zoë felt her spirits lift.

'Her temperature is 35C, Ben,' one of the nurses called and Ben nodded.

'That means she's borderline and that, hopefully, we've caught her in time. We'll go straight to the warm bath and get her temperature up that way. Let's get these clothes off her but leave the hat on.'

Ben immediately set to and helped as the nurses began stripping off the child's clothes. Although most consultants shied away from such menial tasks, Ben never flinched when it came to practicalities. If a job needed doing, he was willing to do it himself and didn't expect everyone to dance attendance on him. Zoë had always admired him for that and discovered that she still admired him for it now, although he possessed so many positive attributes it was hard to pick out one from all the others.

The thought was disquieting bearing in mind that she had no intention of searching out things to admire about him. She followed as Ben picked up little Megan and carried her to the bath. He placed her carefully in the warm water, making sure the whole of her body was immersed apart from her head. The little girl whimpered and opened her eyes and he smiled at her.

'It's all right, poppet. We're just going to make you feel all warm again.'

Zoë felt her eyes fill with tears when she heard the tenderness in his voice. Although Ben was marvellous with all the patients, he was particularly good with any children. He would make the most wonderful father one day and the thought hurt far more than it should have done. She had made up her mind a long time ago that she didn't want children and she wasn't going to change it, not now, not ever.

She took a deep breath and used it to shore up her emotions. She would never be the mother of Ben's children.

CHAPTER THREE

'MEGAN is going to be fine. She's very tired at the moment, which is only to be expected after what's happened, but we don't anticipate any problems.' Ben smiled at the child's anxious parents. 'She'll be going up to the children's ward as soon as a bed is available. We'll keep her in overnight but it's purely a precaution. You should be able to take her home tomorrow.'

Mr and Mrs Turner thanked him profusely and hurried back to their daughter. Ben sighed as he watched them go. 'I can't imagine what they must have been through, can you? Losing a child must be every parent's nightmare.'

He glanced round when Zoë failed to answer and was surprised when he saw how upset she looked. It was rare for Zoë to show her feelings, yet there was no denying that she looked distressed.

'Hey, come on,' he said quickly. 'I know it's upsetting when it's a child involved, but Megan will be fine after a good night's sleep.'

'Of course she will.'

She spun round on her heel, making it clear that she didn't want to discuss the matter, and he sighed. Why had he bothered? He should have known that Zoë wouldn't welcome his concern.

He followed her from ED, pausing on the way out to make sure that Megan's parents had provided the reception staff with all the necessary details. Their family doctor would need to be informed about what had happened, even though there was no reason to suspect that Megan would suffer any repercussions from her adventures. However, it was best to err on the safe side, he'd always found.

Erring on the safe side hadn't achieved very much when it had come to his relationship with Zoë, though, had it? he thought as he left the building. He had done everything he could to make her feel safe and secure, to reassure her that he would never stop loving her. Although he had only the sketchiest idea of her background, she had told him enough to fill in the gaps for himself.

He knew that her parents' divorce must have hit her hard and doubly so when it had meant that she'd been placed in care following her mother's breakdown. However, was it enough to explain why she'd refused to believe that he would never stop loving her? Zoë had been his whole world at one time, yet she had rejected his love, walked away rather than take the risk of trusting him. Although he was over the heartache it had caused him, it was still difficult to understand what she'd done. One thing was certain: no woman was going to put him through the mill again!

Dark thoughts accompanied Ben back to where he had left his car—illegally parked outside ED. He unlocked the doors then paused when Zoë made no attempt to get in. 'I promise I won't make you sit in the back this time,' he said, deliberately opting for levity. The past was the past and he wasn't going to fall into the trap of raking over the embers of their ill-fated affair. 'It's the passenger seat for you, Dr Frost. You've earned it.'

She smiled tightly, not responding to his teasing. 'It's kind of you, Ben, but I'll get a taxi back to the hotel. You live in the opposite direction and I don't want to take you out of your way.'

'I don't mind if you don't,' he replied flippantly, wondering why it seemed so important to get a reaction from her. The days when he had wanted to impress Zoë were long gone. 'It's not as though I have anything better to do with my time seeing as I'm redundant.'

'Redundant?'

'Uh-huh. I feel a bit like Cinderella only I'm the wrong sex.' He looked suitably mournful. 'I'm the best man that nobody wants. I'm not needed for the wedding or for the celebrations that should have come afterwards. It's hard not to feel a little *de trop* in such circumstances.'

'Oh, poor you!' Zoë chuckled, a delicate sound that made the tiny hairs on his neck quiver in appreciation. 'Does nobody love you, then?'

You certainly don't love me, Ben thought, but didn't say so. That would have been a major mistake, a top score on the mistakes Richter scale. The last thing he wanted was to give the impression that he was still hung up on her.

'It looks that way. And that being the case, I may as well run you back to your hotel. At least it will fill in a bit more time and stop me feeling like a reject.'

He got into the car, leaving it to Zoë to decide whether she was going to accept his offer. A frisson ran through him when she slid into the passenger seat but he didn't allow himself to read anything into it. It made no difference if she had opted to spend a bit more time with him.

It was gone seven by the time they drew up outside the hotel. Ben cut the engine, shrugging when Zoë looked questioningly at him. 'I just want to check that nothing untoward has happened with regard to the reception. Ross told me he'd cancelled everything but you never know.'

'Still set on being the perfect best man?' Zoë said lightly, but he heard the tension in her voice and guessed that she was afraid it was merely an excuse to prolong their time together.

Was it? he wondered suddenly. And if so, why? He didn't want her back—no way on earth would he wish for that! It had taken him months to get over her and he wasn't going through that kind of hell again. He'd done what he'd wanted to do, spent the best part of the day with her, and come through it unscathed, so why did he have this niggling feeling that they still had unfinished business? What else did he need to prove? That he was so immune to her he could spend the night with her and walk away in the morning without any regrets?

'I want to be sure that I've carried out my duties to the very best of my ability,' he told her, reeling from the thought.

'Such dedication! I am impressed.'

Zoë laughed and Ben breathed a sigh of relief when it broke the spell. Zoë may have hurt him, but there was no way that he would use her to his own ends like that.

The receptionist must have spotted them coming in because she immediately hurried into the office and reappeared with the manager in tow. Ben's heart sank when he saw how uncomfortable they both looked as he and Zoë approached the desk. He could only conclude that some mishap had occurred relating to the wedding reception. However, the man ignored him and addressed Zoë.

'I'm terribly sorry, Dr Frost, but there's a problem with your room.'

'What sort of problem?' Zoë asked, glancing at the receptionist, who was doing her best to avoid their eyes.

'Unfortunately, a guest on the floor above forgot to turn off the bath taps and the water came through the ceiling of your room.' The manager looked suitably repentant. 'Sadly, the room is too badly damaged for you to spend the night there so I took the liberty of having your belongings moved.'

He lifted a key off its hook and handed it to her. 'Fortunately, we had a cancellation so we were able to move you to a suite. I'm sure you won't be disappointed, Dr Frost. It's our most luxurious accommodation. And by way of apology for the inconvenience you've suffered, we would like to offer you and a guest a complimentary dinner tonight.'

Ben glanced at the key Zoë was holding as the manager scuttled away. All the keys had name tags attached to them and he could read the tag attached to this one without any difficulty. His eyes rose to Zoë's and he was unable to control the smile that twitched the corners of his mouth.

'They say every cloud has a silver lining. If the wedding hadn't been called off, you could have found yourself sleeping on a park bench.'

'Instead of which I'll be sleeping in the Honeymoon Suite.' Zoë looked at the key then burst out laughing. 'I don't believe this is happening!'

'You will when you get to sleep in that fabulous bed,' Ben assured her.

'You've seen the room?' she exclaimed and he sobered abruptly.

'Yes. I came with Ross when he booked it for him and Heather. The manager showed it to us then.'

He took a quick breath but the image of Zoë lying in that huge old-fashioned bed with its muslin canopy filled his head to the exclusion of everything else. It was the room he would have chosen to spend the night in if they'd been getting married, he realised, and the thought was too painful to bear.

'It sounds lovely,' she said softly and he heard an echo of what he was feeling in her voice.

His gaze locked with hers and he felt a shiver run through him. Zoë may have rejected him two years ago but she still wanted him. He could see it in her eyes, see the longing, the yearning, and he understood how she felt because he felt it too. Oh, he hadn't lived like a monk these past two years—far from it. He'd been out with a lot of women, even slept with a few, and it had been fine in a way. However, each and every time he had found himself comparing them to Zoë, and unfavourably too.

He needed to break the cycle, forget what he and Zoë had had, and this may be the only way to do it. If he slept with her tonight, he could rid himself of the last emotional ties. It wouldn't be using her, either, because he could tell it was what she needed too. Zoë needed to draw a line under the past same as he did.

Reaching out, he captured her hand. 'It's a beautiful room, Zoë, the perfect place for two lovers to spend a night. I only wish we could spend tonight there. You and me. Together. It could be our swansong, the perfect ending to what we once meant to each other.'

Soft light filled the room, casting shadows into the corners. Dinner had been served and eaten, although neither of them had done justice to the delicious meal. Zoë caught a glimpse of herself in the window as she drew the curtains and was surprised by how calm she looked, how in control. Inside she was a mess, anticipation making her nerves tingle, her blood heat, her body tremble as though she had a fever. Maybe she did, too, and that's why she had agreed to this. Spending the night with Ben for *any* reason was madness: she knew it and so must he.

She spun round to tell him that she had changed her mind

and stopped. Ben was sitting on the sofa, his eyes closed, his face looking set even in repose. He was as worried as she was about what they were planning and the realisation comforted her in a strange way. Ben was under no illusions. He knew this night would mark the end for them.

The thought left her feeling empty, but she had learned a long time ago how to conquer her emotions. She went over to the couch, sat down and took Ben's hand in hers. His eyelids flickered although he didn't open his eyes. Maybe he needed a second or two more to prepare himself, and she understood. In that respect they were perfectly in tune.

Her heart filled with warmth and if she was honest it also filled with love but that was the most dangerous of all emotions and one she rarely acknowledged. Sliding her fingers between his, she let her palm rest against his, enjoying the warmth of his skin, the shape and strength of his fingers—so different to her own. Ben had such beautiful hands and she had always loved to have him touch her, stroke her, caress her…

Her breath caught on an audible hiss and his eyes opened. Zoë felt a shaft of desire run through her when she saw the expression they held. Ben wanted her. He wanted to make her his and have her make him hers. He wanted it so badly that she could feel his desire for her swirling around them as they sat there, side by side, their fingers entwined.

'Are you sure about this, Zoë? Really sure?' His tone was filled with passion and tenderness in equal measure. Zoë's heart swelled because it was more than she'd expected and far more than she deserved.

'Yes.' Her tone was cool and she felt relieved when she heard it. She was still in control, still able to function on other levels instead of on only the most basic. 'It's what I want, Ben, but are you sure it's what you want?'

'Yes. I'm sure.' He leant forward and brushed her mouth with his lips. 'It's what I need to do.'

He deepened the kiss, effectively cutting short any further discussion, although Zoë would have been hard-pressed to string two words together. It felt as though her brain had stopped functioning, thoughts flitting about her head in no particular order. Her nerve endings were working fine, though, messages zipping back and forth, allowing her to enjoy every moment of the kiss, to savour their closeness, to revel in the desire that had risen inside her like a hot tide.

She gave a little murmur as she wrapped her arms around his neck and drew his head down so that she could kiss him back with equal fervour. She heard him groan as her lips parted, felt the hot sweet rush of pleasure when his tongue slid inside her mouth and groaned too because it was an overture to what would come later. When his hands slid down her sides, following the curves of her breasts, the dip of her waist, the swell of her hips, she shuddered. Just the feel of his hands through her clothes was enough to incite her passion.

He drew back, resting his forehead against hers as he dragged in several rough breaths that made his chest rise and fall enticingly against her breasts. Zoë could feel her nipples harden as the muscles in his torso brushed against them, and sighed. She'd always been embarrassingly responsive where Ben was concerned and nothing had changed.

'Wow! I know I should come up with something more erudite, but that sums it up better than anything else. A great big fat wow!'

'Then I suppose wow will have to do.' Zoë laughed, wondering how she'd forgotten what fun Ben could be even in the throes of passion. Tilting back her head, she regarded him through narrowed eyes, enjoying the fact that she felt comfort-

able enough to tease him. 'Think about this very carefully
before you reply. Was the kiss as good as it used to be?'

'Better,' he said firmly, taking her back into his arms and
holding her so close that she could feel his heart beating in coun-
terpoint to hers. 'The fact that we're no longer under such
pressure to make our relationship work makes all the difference.'

Zoë wasn't sure what to make of that idea but he didn't give
her time to dwell on it. When he pressed his lips to the corner
of her mouth, she relaxed against him, giving herself up to the
delight of being in his arms again. He kissed every inch of her
face and her neck then started to work his way down her body,
unhooking buttons and unzipping zips, easing her out of her
clothes with so little fuss that it was a moment before she
realised that all she had on was a pair of panties and they were
soon dispensed with.

'You're very good at this undressing lark,' she whispered,
feeling decidedly overexposed seeing as Ben was still wearing
his clothes.

'Aren't I just?' His handsome face filled with laughter as he
planted a kiss on her nose. 'I've had a lot of practice.'

'Thanks to all the women you've undressed lately,' she
muttered, not appreciating the thought of Ben and a series of
unknown women in various states of undress.

'No, thanks to all the *patients* I've undressed.' He kissed her
again, looking a little smug about getting a rise out of her.

'You have nurses to do that for you,' she retorted, resenting
his teasing and what had prompted it. She had no right to feel
jealous at the thought of him and other women when she had
rejected him, but she did.

'I do.' He smiled into her eyes. 'But I've always preferred a
hands-on approach, if you remember?'

She remembered all right, recalled in glorious detail what

his hands could do—exactly what they were doing now. Zoë closed her eyes as she felt his clever fingers stroking her skin and setting off a whole chain of reactions. When he ran the tip of his finger down the hollow between her breasts, she gasped. When he let it trail across her right nipple, she moaned. When it found her belly button and dipped in and out, she wriggled invitingly because she knew where it would be heading next.

The thought sent a rush of desire coursing through her, a feeling she hadn't experienced in very a long time. Although she had no intention of letting Ben know it, she hadn't slept with anyone else in the past two years. She'd had offers, of course—several highly personable men, doctors she worked with in Paris, had asked her out, but she had refused their invitations. She'd told herself that she hadn't wanted any complications in her life, but now she realised the truth was far more complex: she hadn't wanted anyone except Ben.

Tears filled her eyes as he lifted her into his arms and carried her into the bedroom. He laid her down on the huge old-fashioned bed with a gentleness that spoke volumes about the man he was. Ben had loved her, cared for her, wanted only for her to be happy. She'd known that and had fought against it. If she had accepted what he'd wanted to give her, she would never have been able to leave him, never been able to bear it if he'd left her.

She had rejected him because she'd been afraid, not because she hadn't loved him. Everyone she had ever loved had let her down—her mother, her father, everyone—and she'd been terrified that Ben would do the same. She had tried to explain that to him, but it had been too difficult for him to understand and in the end she'd had no choice but to leave him rather than run the risk of being hurt again. However, as he stripped off his clothes and came to lie beside her under the canopy of muslin clouds, Zoë knew that he was the only man she would ever love. She had given Ben her heart even if he didn't know it. And if she couldn't have Ben, she didn't want anyone else.

CHAPTER FOUR

March

'THIS guy's got a ruptured spleen. Get on to the surgical team and tell them we need someone down here now, not in an hour's time!'

Ben rapped out the order, ignoring the look his staff exchanged. His temper had been on a knife edge for weeks and he didn't need a psychologist to tell him why. He'd been deluding himself by thinking he could draw a line under the past by sleeping with Zoë. What it had done had been to arouse a lot of emotions he'd thought he had buried. If only he'd had the sense to realise the risk he'd been taking.

He gritted his teeth because he refused to go down the *if-only* route again. He'd made a mistake and that was that. Now he had to get on with his life. Turning to Jo Morris, the senior staff nurse on duty that day, he deliberately moderated his tone.

'Can you check how the passenger in that car is doing, Jo? She was complaining of chest pains when she was brought in. If they haven't settled down, she's going to need an ECG.'

'Will do.'

Jo gave him a smile before she hurried out of Resus, leaving him feeling guiltier than ever. Although there may have been a few funny looks exchanged, everyone had put up with his bad temper with remarkably good grace. It made him realise how lucky he was to have such a tolerant group of people around him.

Unlooping his stethoscope from around his neck, he bent over the patient again. Brian Roberts had been cycling to work when he had been hit by a car. According to an eyewitness, the vehicle had rammed straight into him. Brian had suffered a range of injuries, the most serious being a ruptured spleen. He was losing a lot of blood and Ben was anxious to get him to Theatre as quickly as possible.

'What did Surgical have to say?' he asked when Adam Sanders, their senior house officer, came hurrying back.

'They've promised that s-someone will be here in the next five minutes,' Adam informed him, stammering a little in case Ben thought that wasn't soon enough. He'd been on the receiving end of Ben's tongue for most of the day, a fact that Ben now bitterly regretted.

'Excellent. Obviously, you've managed to gee them up where others have failed,' he said heartily, pleased to see that Adam immediately perked up. He nodded to the patient, wanting to continue smoothing the young doctor's ruffled feathers. 'Have a listen to his chest. I think the right lung sounds a bit dodgy—what do you think?'

Adam turned bright pink at having his opinion canvassed and listened intently to the patient's chest. 'It sounds a bit rough to me, too. Maybe there's a build-up of fluid,' he suggested, emboldened by Ben's more reasonable attitude.

'I agree.' Ben nodded. 'He took a real knock when he came off his bike, which accounts for the ruptured spleen. If a rib was fractured as well, it could have caused bleeding into the pleural cavity.' He turned to Abby Blake, another of their nurses, who was standing off to one side. 'I'd like a chest drain set, please, Abby.'

It didn't take long to draw off the excess fluid that had collected in the pleural cavity. Ben had just finished when the surgical reg arrived and whisked the patient away, tutting his displeasure as though it was ED's fault that there'd been a delay. Ben stripped off his gloves and tossed them into the bin.

'That was a good job, folks. Thank you.'

'Oh, so we're out of the doghouse now, are we?' Abby piped up. She grinned at him. 'About time too. We were this close to mutiny.'

She held her first finger and thumb a scant quarter inch apart and Ben laughed.

'Am I supposed to be worried? Now, if you were this close.' He pressed his thumb and finger tightly together. 'I might be *really* concerned, but not when I have so much leeway!'

Everyone laughed and it went a long way to restoring the harmony that was such an important part of them working as a team. Ben made himself a promise that he would stop behaving like a jerk from now on as he left Resus. There was no point regretting what had happened with Zoë. He'd taken a chance and it hadn't paid off. He'd coped with worse *and* survived to tell the tale, too. One thing was certain: Zoë wasn't wasting her time thinking about him.

It took Zoë almost three hours to drive from the airport to Dalverston and she was exhausted by the time she got there. An accident on the M6 motorway had caused a huge tailback of traffic and it was a relief when she reached her exit. She parked in the hotel's car park and hurried inside, filling in the registration card the receptionist gave her with a hand that trembled from a mixture of tiredness and emotion. So much had happened since the night she'd stayed here with Ben.

Fear ran coldly through her and she hastily took the key off the receptionist, shaking her head when the girl asked if she needed a porter to deal with her luggage. All she'd brought with her was an overnight case and she could manage that herself. She took the lift to the third floor and let herself into the room, barely glancing around to check that everything was as it should be. She was here and that was the main thing, although what happened from here on was a question she couldn't answer. It all depended on Ben and how he reacted to what she had to tell him. It was a lot to expect of him, probably too much bearing in mind what had gone on before. But he was the only person she could ask for help. If he refused, she had no idea what she was going to do.

Ben was stepping out of the shower the following morning when the phone rang and for a moment he was tempted to ignore it. It was his day off, the first one he'd had for weeks, and he really didn't want to have to go in to work. He sighed as he snatched a towel off the rail. If he didn't answer it, he'd spend the day wondering how the department was coping. Talk about being trapped between a rock and a hard place!

'Ben Nicholls.' He hunched his shoulder to keep the receiver against his ear while he rubbed himself dry. If it was the hospital, he would need to get there asap. The kind of injuries they dealt with weren't the sort that could wait for any length of time.

'Ben, it's Zoë.'

The receiver slid off his shoulder and landed with a crash on the floor. Ben cursed as he picked it up. He must be hallucinating. He could have sworn the caller had said she was Zoë.

'Sorry about that. I dropped the receiver,' he said briskly, dismissing the idea. No way would Zoë be phoning him at this hour of the morning… Correction: no way would Zoë be phoning him at *any* hour of the day.

'It's OK. Look, Ben, if I've caught you at a bad time I can

phone back later, but I really need to speak to you. Is there any chance that we can meet up sometime today?'

Ben's breath caught because there was no mistaking Zoë's voice this time. 'It really is you, Zoë?'

'Of course it is. So when can we meet? I wouldn't pester you, Ben, but it's imperative that I talk to you.'

Ben frowned when he heard how uptight she sounded. It was obvious that something must have happened to bring her back to Dalverston, although he had no idea what it could be. 'Of course we can meet. I've got today off as it happens so name the time and the place and I'll be there.'

'Ten o'clock in the lounge of the hotel,' she said quickly and he knew that she must have rehearsed her answer in advance.

'Fine. Can you tell me what this is all about? I mean, it's a bit sudden, you turning up like this…'

'I'd prefer to wait until later. Ten o'clock it is.'

She hung up before he could finish what he'd been saying, leaving him feeling more perplexed than ever. The fact that Zoë had flown back to England to arrange this meeting didn't make sense. After all, he'd had no contact with her since December. There'd been no phone calls, no notes, not even a Christmas card—*nada*. The fact that he hadn't phoned or written to her either was by the by—he wasn't foolish enough to do that.

No, Zoë had made it clear after that night they'd spent together that she didn't want to see him again, which made her arrival all the more puzzling. What could be so urgent that she needed to speak to him when she'd ignored him for the past three months?

Ben blinked as the words resounded inside his head: it had been three months since he and Zoë had slept together. Was it possible that she had come to tell him she was pregnant?

Shock coursed through every vein in his body, turned his legs to jelly, and he collapsed onto the bed. He hadn't used a condom that night. Zoë had told him that she was on the Pill to regulate her menstrual cycle and there was no need for them to take extra precautions. However, everyone knew that the Pill wasn't one hundred per cent effective—no method of contraception was apart from abstinence. Maybe, just maybe, their night together had resulted in a baby, their baby, his and Zoë's child.

Ben closed his eyes as his head began to reel. He could barely take it in and knew he needed time to think about it, then realised in a flash there was nothing to think about. If Zoë *was* having his baby, it was the most wonderful thing that could have happened. One thing was certain, too: he intended to be there for his child every step of the way!

Zoë chose her seat with care, opting for a table in the corner from where she could see the door. She needed to be in control if she hoped to get through this meeting and didn't need any surprises like Ben appearing without her realising it…

Her breath caught when she saw him coming in. Despite the chill in the air, all he was wearing was a thin sweater and jeans. Had he dragged on the first clothes that had come to hand? Dressed in a hurry because he hadn't wanted to keep her waiting? It was so typical of his thoughtfulness, of the caring man he was, and the thought eased some of her tension a little. Ben wouldn't let her down. She knew it.

'Thanks for coming,' she said quietly as he sat down. 'I've ordered coffee. It should be here in a minute.'

'Fine.' He leant forward and she could see the lines of tension on his face. 'What's this all about, Zoë?'

'Let's wait for the coffee, shall we? I could do with a cup and I'm sure you could too.'

Ben couldn't hide his impatience as he subsided back in the

chair, but he didn't push her and she was grateful for that. It seemed to take for ever before the waitress arrived with their tray, although in truth it was only a few minutes. Zoë picked up the heavy silver pot and poured them both a cup of the steaming brew, automatically adding milk and sugar to Ben's cup before handing it to him. He had a sweet tooth, something she had often teased him about.

'Thanks.'

He took a sip of his coffee then set the cup and saucer on the table and rubbed his hands together. Zoë realised with a start how nervous he looked and wished that she hadn't added to the pressure by making him wait those extra few minutes. Putting down her own cup, she sat up straighter. It would be easier for them both if she told him what she wanted rather than draw it out.

'Are you pregnant, Zoë?'

The question caught her off guard. Her eyes flew to his face but it was impossible to tell what he was thinking. He was deliberately masking his feelings and the thought made her shiver because it proved that the dynamics of their relationship had changed dramatically. The Ben she remembered would never have been so guarded around her; she would have known immediately how he was feeling. Obviously she didn't know him as well as she'd thought and may have been wrong to assume that he would help her.

Fear rushed through her and she half rose, but Ben was too quick for her. He caught her hand, shaking his head when she tried to free herself. 'I'm not letting you run away without answering my question. I may have got it completely wrong, but it's the only thing that makes any sense. You're having my baby, aren't you, Zoë? Why else would you have come here to see me?'

Zoë sank back into the chair when she heard the pain in his voice. She had hurt him badly and it was the one thing she had tried to avoid. All she could do now was be truthful and hope that in some small way it would make up for what she had done. Raising her head, she looked him in the eyes.

'Yes, I'm pregnant, and, before you ask, Ben, it is your child. It couldn't be anyone else's. I haven't slept with anyone else since we split up.'

A dozen different emotions chased across his face before he got himself under control. 'I see. So you must be, what? Eleven, twelve weeks?'

'Almost thirteen,' she replied without hesitation because she had been keeping track of every day.

'And do you intend to keep the baby?'

Zoë winced at his bluntness, but there was no point in lying by claiming that having a termination hadn't crossed her mind. The only way this would work was if she was completely honest with him and even then it may be too much to expect.

'Yes. Having a child has never been on my agenda, as you know. However, I've decided to keep the baby.'

'I see.' His brows rose. 'That does surprise me. I didn't think you would change your mind about something like this. I assume you've thought about how it could impact on your career?'

Zoë flushed when she heard the edge in his voice. Ben had never agreed with her decision to put her career first. They'd had many an argument about it, in fact. However, what he hadn't understood was that it wasn't just the fact that her career would have needed to be put on a back burner if she'd had a baby to look after. It had been more complicated than that, bound up with her childhood and her fear of inflicting the same kind of heartache on her child that she had suffered. All of a sudden Zoë found herself wishing that she had explained it all before, but it was too late now. Now she had to deal with the biggest and most terrifying decision she had ever faced.

'I have, and I still intend to have this baby. It's what I want, Ben, and I hope it's what you want, too. I know this must be a shock for you…'

'That's an understatement!'

He gave a harsh laugh that cut her to the quick. He sounded so bitter, so unlike the Ben she knew. Once again fear curled coldly in the pit of her stomach but she had to remember that she was doing this for her child. Their child. And she could only do it with his help.

'I'm sorry. I didn't plan on this happening. As I told you at the time, I was on the Pill, but I'd had a stomach bug a few days before I flew over for the wedding, and I suppose that's what messed things up.'

'I understand, Zoë. These things happen and that really isn't the issue.' He shook his head when she went to interrupt. 'No, hear me out.'

Zoë nodded, although she couldn't help wishing that he sounded more like the old Ben. He seemed so much sterner and it worried her when she'd told him only part of what he needed to know. It was the major part, the one that would most closely involve him, but she knew that when she told him the rest he would be shocked. All she could hope was that, no matter how it appeared, he hadn't completely stopped caring about her.

The thought was almost too poignant. Zoë pushed it to the farthest reaches of her mind as he continued. 'I may be shocked to learn that I'm about to become a father but I'm pleased too. I've never made any secret of the fact that I want kids, although I rather hoped I'd have a wife before they came along.' He gave her one of his trademark grins. 'I'm a bit of a traditionalist at heart. You can blame my mother for that.'

Zoë smiled in relief. 'So long as you're pleased.'

'Oh, I am.' He reached across the table and captured her hands. 'It's wonderful news, even if we didn't plan on it happening.'

He squeezed her fingers and Zoë shivered. She'd not allowed herself to think about that night they'd spent together but when Ben touched her like this, she couldn't help remembering how wonderful it had been. They may have slept together to mark the end of their relationship, but it had been a magical experience. It seemed fitting that it was then they had created this new life growing inside her, a tiny memento of the occasion which she was desperate to protect.

Zoë took a deep breath, feeling the certainty of what she was doing chase away her fears. She was willing to give up her own life for the sake of this precious child.

Ben could hear his own heart beating. Every time he spoke it was to the accompaniment of a sound like a big bass drum thumping in the background. There should have been trumpets too, he thought, playing a fanfare so they could turn this into a real celebration. He was going to become a dad! What more joyous occasion was there to celebrate than that?

He took a steadying breath and got his euphoria back on its leash. Wonderful though this news was, it didn't change the situation. Zoë may have come to tell him about the baby but it had been out of a sense of duty and not because she wanted them to get back together. He didn't want that either. She'd hurt him too much to willingly take such a risk again.

'I'm glad you're pleased, Ben.'

She withdrew her hands and Ben felt a chill slide down his spine when he saw the expression in her eyes. It wasn't so much that she was deliberately distancing herself from him—he was used to that. It was the hint of something else he saw there, a kind of wariness or fear even, that made him grow tense.

If he wasn't mistaken, Zoë had something else to tell him apart from this piece of news.

'What haven't you told me?' he demanded. 'Come on, Zoë, out with it. You're holding something back, aren't you?'

'Yes.' She looked down at her hands for a moment and then raised her head. 'Two days after I realised I was pregnant, I discovered a lump in my left breast. I've had all the tests and there's absolutely no doubt about the diagnosis. I have cancer, Ben, and I'm going to need treatment for it, which is where I hope you'll come in. I'm going to need your help to look after this baby.'

CHAPTER FIVE

ZOË saw the colour drain from Ben's face. She wished with all her heart that there'd been a gentler way to break the news to him but nothing she could have said would have prepared him.

'I don't know what to say… Hell, I don't know what to *think* even!'

He stood up and strode out of the hotel but Zoë didn't go after him. He needed to work this out himself, decide if he could commit to helping her. Having a child was one thing; having a child with a woman who had a life-threatening illness was something entirely different. She wouldn't blame him if he decided to opt out.

A sob rose to her throat but she forced it down. She wouldn't be able to cope if she gave in to the fear gnawing at her insides. She had to remain strong if her baby was to survive. Automatically, she laid her hand on the curve of her stomach. Her pregnancy was just starting to show, her waist thickening, her breasts growing fuller and heavier. The baby inside her didn't care if she had cancer—it simply wanted to survive and she intended to give it the best chance possible. That had been the driving force behind her recent decisions. Once she'd discovered it was possible to continue with the pregnancy, she'd known it was what she wanted to do. She was going to give this precious child a chance of life, no matter what it cost her.

'Tell me everything, right from the beginning.'

All of a sudden Ben was back, looking so in control that it was scary to see the change in him. However, Zoë guessed it was the only way he could deal with what she'd told him and didn't resent it. It didn't matter how he felt about her so long as he promised to take care of their child. She stood up. 'Let's go up to my room. It's a little too public in here for this sort of conversation.'

Ben didn't say a word as he followed her to the lift. They rode up in silence, neither of them seemingly having any desire to speak. Unlocking the door to her room, Zoë ushered him inside, pointing to the armchair beside the window.

'You have that. I'll sit on the bed.'

Ben walked over to the chair although he didn't sit down. He waited until she had seated herself then looked at her. 'OK, so what happened exactly?'

'As I told you, I found a lump in my breast one morning when I was in the shower. It was about the size of a pea, very hard and regular. I did wonder if it had something to do with me being pregnant but in the end it simply didn't feel right.'

'So you went for tests?'

'Yes. My doctor told me it was probably a cyst but just to be on the safe side she sent me for a biopsy. She wasn't keen on me having a mammogram because of the danger to the baby so we bypassed that stage.'

'And the biopsy came back positive?'

'Yes. It was a shock, yet I think I had prepared myself for bad news so it didn't hit me as hard as it might have done. It was a stage 1 tumour and the surgeon removed it with a lumpectomy.'

'You've already started treatment!' he exclaimed.

'I had the operation two weeks ago. Obviously, having a general anaesthetic presented a risk for the baby. However, I've had a scan since then and my obstetrician is confident that everything is fine.'

'I thought the usual procedure was to terminate a pregnancy when it's discovered the mother has cancer,' he cut in.

'It is. My doctor tried to persuade me to have a termination but I decided against it.'

'You were willing to balance your chances of survival against that of your unborn child,' he said slowly. 'That's what it may come down to in the end, Zoë, and that's what puzzles me. You've never wanted children so why take such a risk with your life?'

'Because when I discovered I could be left infertile after the treatment, it changed my perceptions of what I want from life.' Tears trickled down her cheeks before she could stop them. 'This could be my one and only chance of having a baby, and I don't want to lose it.'

'Don't!' He knelt in front of her, gathering her into his arms while he rocked her to and fro, and Zoë cried all the harder. She'd been so shocked and so scared, and it had been so hard to face what was happening on her own.

She cried until she had no more tears left and felt much better for it. She had been bottling up her emotions for weeks and it felt good to get them out into the open. It also felt marvellous to have Ben there, holding her and making her feel so wonderfully safe.

She gently freed herself, knowing that she couldn't let him hold her any longer. She needed his help for the sake of their child but she hadn't changed her mind about what *she* needed. She loved him but she wasn't going to risk having her heart broken. She couldn't cope with that on top of everything else.

She stood up and went to the dressing-table, plucking a

tissue out of the box and wiping her eyes. Ben was sitting on the chair and he smiled as she sat down on the bed.

'Feel better now?'

'Yes, thank you.'

She dredged up a smile, aware of how stilted she sounded. Keeping him at arm's length had never been easy and it was more difficult than ever now, but she had to do it. She couldn't let him take over her life, care for her as well as their child. What if he grew tired of the responsibility, then how would she cope? To allow herself to feel safe and secure only to have it all snatched away would be too much to bear.

'So what happens next? You've had a lumpectomy and I imagine the next stage is chemo.' He frowned. 'How will chemotherapy affect the baby? It must pose a risk to the child, yet you can't *not* have it because of the risk to you.'

'I've done a lot of research in the past few weeks, and had a lot of advice from various experts, too,' she assured him, focussing on the practicalities rather than how she felt. 'The opinion is that so long as chemotherapy doesn't begin until the end of the first trimester—around fourteen weeks—the baby is unlikely to be harmed in any way.'

'But being pregnant must present more of a risk for you. What about all the extra hormones that are whizzing around your system—surely they will exacerbate the problem?'

'I was concerned about that too, but I got in touch with an oncologist in London and he assured me that being pregnant won't make any difference.' She gave a little shrug because it was hard to talk about this and remain unemotional. 'Basically, being pregnant won't shorten my life and if I have a termination it won't lengthen it either. My cancer will follow its course and that's that.'

Ben looked down at the floor and she could tell that he was struggling to deal with what he was hearing. It was a lot for him to take in on top of learning that he was to be a father. Leaning over, she touched his hand.

'I'm sorry, Ben. I wish I didn't have to tell you all this. I know what a shock it must be for you and I apologise for that.'

He lifted his head and looked into her eyes. 'There's nothing to apologise for, Zoë. You didn't ask for this to happen. I only wish I knew of a way to make it go away.'

'I wish you did too,' she said softly, touched by the sincerity in his voice. Maybe Ben had changed in many ways but inside he was still the same deeply compassionate man she had always admired and loved.

The thought was too painful. She could have found real happiness if she'd accepted what Ben had been offering her, stopped fighting her feelings and admitted that she had loved him too. If she had faced her fears, they could have been together for ever... Or for however long she had left in this world.

A cold chill enveloped her. She had no idea how long for ever would be, had she? She might have years ahead of her but, equally, she might have only months and nobody could tell her which it would be. Could she really have borne to watch Ben suffer if her treatment failed?

She let go of his hands, mentally and physically distancing herself even though it was incredibly hard to do so. Ben had never blamed her for her inability to accept his love. Oh, he had tried to change her mind—many times! But he'd never blamed her and it was typical of him, what made him the man he was. He had put her first and, if she'd let him, he always would have done so too. Now all she wanted was that he put that same love and dedication into caring for their child.

Ben got up and went to the window, needing a moment to collect himself. What Zoë had told him had knocked him for six. He may have worked hard to get over her but that didn't alter how he felt at this moment. The thought of a world without Zoë in it didn't bear thinking about.

His heart shuddered as he turned to her but he refused to let her see how afraid he felt. If she could deal with this with fortitude, so could he. 'When exactly are you starting your chemotherapy?' he asked, relieved to hear that he sounded almost normal.

'In two weeks' time. I'm booked into the Clinique des Bois on the fifteenth.'

Ben frowned. 'You're having your treatment in France?'

'Of course. Where else would I have it?'

'Here, of course. I thought that was why you'd come back to Dalverston.'

'Not at all. I'll be having my treatment in Paris.'

'But you said that you needed my help?' he said roughly, and heard her sigh.

'With the baby, Ben. Sorry. I didn't make myself clear.'

'You didn't.' He sat down again. 'I don't understand, Zoë. How can I help with the baby if you're living in Paris?'

'You can't, not at the moment anyway.' She hurried on when he looked blankly at her. 'If anything happens to me, Ben, I want to be sure that our baby will be taken care of. It's a lot to ask but if I know that you're willing to bring up our child, I'll feel so much easier.'

'If anything happens…' He stopped and swallowed but there seemed to be a lump in his throat the size of Ayers Rock. Zoë expected him to look after their child if she died? What she didn't want was him to be involved *before* that event.

Anger rose so swiftly inside him that he had no time to control it. 'How dare you cut me out like that? I know you don't give a damn about me, Zoë, but at least I thought you had some respect for me.'

'Ben!' She shot to her feet when he rose. Ben could see the shock on her face and part of him regretted his outburst. Zoë didn't need this on top of everything else she had to contend with, but he couldn't help himself. Zoë didn't want *him*. She just wanted him to take over if anything happened to *her*.

'Ben, please. I don't understand what's wrong. I never meant to upset you…'

'I'm sure you didn't. You wanted to avoid any kind of emotional upset, didn't you? Well, I'm sorry, Zoë, but that isn't going to happen. I intend to play an active part in my child's life. I intend to be there for him or her every step of the way, from conception through to birth, and beyond. What I don't intend to be is some sort of stopgap who will pick up the pieces if you die.'

He saw her blanch at his bluntness but he refused to compromise. Maybe Zoë thought she didn't need his help but he knew differently. She had weeks of gruelling treatment ahead of her and she needed all the support she could get.

'So what do you propose?' she said in a tiny little voice that cut him to the quick.

'That you come back to Dalverston and undergo your treatment here.'

'But I work in Paris—how will I manage if I come back here?' she protested. 'I need to earn a living, Ben.'

'There's a vacancy in ED. It's only temporary while one of the staff recovers from surgery, but it's yours if you want it. As for where you'll live, you can stay at my flat. There's two bedrooms so you won't feel compromised in any way.'

She flushed. 'I really don't think that will be an issue, do you?' She didn't give him time to reply, which was probably a good thing. Ben didn't want to think about how it would be, having her live with him. He groaned. If he was overcome with lust, he would just have to deal with it!

'I'm not sure, Ben. It just seems simpler if I stay in Paris as I'd planned.'

'And what happens if you find that you can't cope by yourself, or that you feel too ill to work?' he said, knowing that he had to convince her to see sense. The thought of her going through this ordeal on her own was too much—he had to make her understand that it was crazy even to contemplate it.

'It may not come to that,' she countered but he saw the fear in her eyes and knew that her bravery was merely a front. Underneath, she was scared to death and she had every right to be too.

He leant forward, holding her gaze. 'I hope it doesn't, Zoë, but you don't know how you're going to feel once your chemo kicks in. It's hard enough just being pregnant and holding down a demanding job, but when you factor in the rest… Well.'

'It's a big step, moving back here,' she whispered.

'Yes, but no bigger than the step you took when you left. You'll have a job and somewhere to live, people who care about you and who want to help you. You aren't running away now, Zoë. You're ill and you need all the support you can get. That's all I want to do, help you any way I can.'

'And take care of our baby,' she said softly, her eyes staring into his. 'He or she is the most important thing in all of this.'

'Of course.' Ben wasn't sure if he agreed with that sentiment but he didn't say so. He didn't want to admit to himself let alone Zoë how devastated he would be if anything happened to her. 'By taking care of you, we'll be taking care of the baby too.'

'And if anything does happen to me, if…if my treatment isn't successful, you promise that you'll always love and care for it?'

Tears burned his eyes as he nodded. 'You know I will. I shall love this child and do everything in my power to make sure that he or she is safe and happy.'

'All right, then, I'll do what you ask and come back to Dalverston.'

She turned away but not before he'd seen the glisten of tears on her lashes too. The urge to take her in his arms and comfort her was overwhelming but he knew it would be a mistake, not because she might reject him—he could handle that. But because it might upset her even more and he couldn't bear that, not when she was trying so hard to be brave.

He got up and went to the door, his body aching with a pain that ran bone-deep. He'd thought he was over her but it certainly didn't feel that way. 'You must be worn out. I'll leave you to rest and speak to you tonight.'

'I'm flying back to Paris tonight,' she told him and he sighed. It was clear that she had allowed herself the minimum amount of time to persuade him to fall in with her plans. If he hadn't agreed, she would have returned to Paris and that would have been the end of the matter.

'I'll drive you to the airport, then. What time does your flight leave?'

'Seven o'clock but you don't need to drive me there. I hired a car and I'll have to return it.'

'Fine.' He could sense the barriers going up and knew he needed to back off. He'd won a major battle and he could afford to concede this skirmish if it made her feel less threatened. 'Give me your Paris phone number and I'll be in touch. It will take a few days to get everything sorted out, I imagine, but you should be back here…when? Next week, the week after that?'

'I'm not sure.' She stood up straighter. 'I hadn't planned on this, Ben.'

'Neither had I, but we're both going to have to learn to adapt, aren't we?' He knew that sounded harsh but he wasn't going to give in and let her go her own sweet way, struggling to cope on her own, and she had to accept that. Her shoulders slumped as she turned away and started to straighten the bedspread.

'I'll let you know when to expect me.'

'Thank you. I'll let the hospital know that you're taking that job.'

He left it there, afraid that if he lingered he would do something stupid like break down and weep. He needed to be strong for Zoë's sake, for their baby's sake, for…

Tears were suddenly streaming down his face as he walked along the corridor to the lift. He knew how devastated he would feel if anything happened to her.

CHAPTER SIX

'THIS is Jo Morris, senior sister on ED, and Adam Sanders, our senior house officer.'

Zoë said hello, replying politely to the friendly greetings. She remembered seeing the pair when she and Ben had rescued that child from the hills. It seemed an age ago now, although in truth it must be only a matter of months. She'd had no idea then that her life would take such a dramatic turn.

She pushed the thought to the back of her mind as she followed Ben into Resus. He was giving her the grand tour, making sure she knew where everything was kept. Although she'd worked there before, it was easy to forget where vital pieces of equipment were kept. The last thing Ben needed in an emergency was her bumbling around the place.

'That just about covers it. Most things are where they used to be, although there's been a few changes since your time, mainly to the staff. We've lost a lot of good folk, I'm sorry to say.'

Ben grimaced, his handsome face looking unusually stern in the bright glare of the lights. She knew that he was deliberately keeping everything on a professional footing and she was grateful for that. It would help to alleviate the strain if they could stick to their roles as colleagues while they were in the hospital.

Her heart jerked as she thought about what would happen away from there. She had already moved into Ben's flat. She'd flown back from Paris the previous day and he had met her at the airport. She'd lived in rented accommodation in Paris so at least she hadn't had any furniture to ship back to England, but there'd still been an awful lot of stuff. Fortunately, Ben had hired a van but she had managed to fill it with her belongings and now they were littered about his flat. She couldn't help feeling guilty for invading his space.

'Keeping hold of good staff is a major undertaking,' she said quietly, sticking to their current remit. 'We had the same problem in Paris—you no sooner hired someone decent than someone else left.'

'It seems to be a universal problem,' he agreed, opening the door for her. 'We have a number of staff from overseas working here while others have left to take up positions abroad.'

'They say the grass is always greener on the other side,' she replied lightly, heading back to the cubicles.

'So they do.' Ben put a hand on her arm. 'What's happening about your chemo? Have you been given a start date yet? The oncology department did promise to get in touch with you.'

'They did, and I start my treatment the Monday after next.' Zoë took a deep breath to control the fear that made her stomach churn each time she thought about what she had to face. 'Deborah Gaston is my consultant. She has a particular interest in cases like mine, apparently. She will be liaising with the obstetrics consultant, although I don't know his name.'

'Daniel Walker,' Ben supplied helpfully. 'He took over at the beginning of the year and he's very good, too. You'll be in safe hands from what I've heard.'

'Good.'

Zoë smiled to allay the impression that she was concerned,

although she doubted if Ben was fooled. She sighed as she collected the next patient's admission notes. Ben knew her too well and there was very little she would be able to keep from him. It was worrying to know how vulnerable she was going to be in the next few months but she had to deal with it the best way she could. So long as she didn't allow him to take over her life, she should be fine.

There was the usual run of minor injuries—sprains, cuts, a sore throat that should have been dealt with by the patient's GP—and the morning flew by. She was about to go for lunch when the outer doors opened and a young man staggered in, clutching his chest and groaning loudly. Zoë hurried forward and reached him just as he keeled over. Moving his hand out of the way, she gasped in dismay when she saw the handle of a knife sticking out of his chest.

'Can I have some help over here?' she shouted. 'I need a trolley as well, stat!'

Everybody whizzed into action and a trolley appeared along with Jo and Adam and a male nurse whose name Zoë couldn't remember. Zoë stood up, glancing at the others as she took hold of the young man's left arm and shoulder. 'On my count…'

'I'll do that.'

All of a sudden Ben was there, moving her aside as he took her place. Zoë didn't have time to protest as the team lifted the young man onto the trolley and rushed him through to Resus. Ben glanced at her as she hurried after them, his face set.

'You shouldn't be lifting anything heavy at the moment. If you need help, you're to ask. Got it?'

Zoë knew he was right, but it was galling to have restrictions imposed on her. 'I don't need people fussing over me.'

'Nobody's fussing, Zoë. It's common sense—that's all.'

They'd reached Resus by then and he didn't say anything else as they wheeled the trolley through the doors. Zoë tagged along in its wake, feeling like a spare part. If she was only to be allowed to treat the minor injuries—the cuts and bruises—it wasn't on. Either she was good enough to do her job, or she wasn't.

There was a light of battle in her eyes as she stepped forward. Ben looked at her, his eyes meeting hers across the trolley, and there was a firmness about his expression that she had rarely seen there before. Zoë realised there was no point arguing when he was determined to have his own way.

'As soon as we get him onto the bed, I want you to monitor his breathing, Zoë. From the position that knife has entered his chest, we could be dealing with a haemothorax and I want it sorted out sooner rather than later.' He turned to the others. 'OK, let's get a move on.'

The patient was transferred to the bed and everyone sprang into action. Jo started to cut off his clothes, Adam began setting up the monitoring equipment and the male nurse—Jason, Zoë suddenly remembered—grabbed a handful of plastic aprons and distributed them to everyone present. Zoë put on her apron then unwound her stethoscope from around her neck. The patient's breathing was very laboured and when she checked his lung sounds, she realised that Ben was right. There was blood in the pleural cavity and it would need to be removed.

She told him her findings, unsurprised when he merely nodded. He didn't look for kudos for having made such an excellent diagnosis. That wasn't his way. He never sought compliments, never tried to bolster his ego in any way, shape or form. It was one of the things she had admired about him and she admired it still—his confidence, his certainty, his humanity. He was a good man, a kind man, a dedicated doctor and a person people instinctively relied on.

She could so easily rely on him too, and she was going to

have to do so to a certain extent for the sake of their child. What she mustn't do was let herself rely on him to get through the next few difficult months. In her heart she knew that if she let herself lean on Ben, she wouldn't be able to stop, wouldn't be able to prevent her heart being broken when he grew tired of the responsibility, as he was bound to do.

It was different with their child. Ben adored children and she knew that he would never grow tired of looking after their son or their daughter, unlike her own father. But she could become a burden to him because of her illness and she didn't want to be that. No, she either kept her distance or she gave him her all and she knew which it had to be. There could be no in-between where Ben was concerned.

The young man's name was Ryan Andrews. He was nineteen years old and a student at the local college. Jo discovered all that from what the boy had on him—a wallet containing his driver's licence, a student card and a letter from his parents who lived in Dorset. Ben nodded when the sister told him what she'd found.

'You need to tell the police. I take it that someone has phoned them?'

'Ruth said she'd do it,' Jo confirmed, referring to their receptionist.

'Good. Can you check if there's a police officer in Reception? The sooner they get in touch with his parents the better.'

Jo didn't ask why. She didn't need to. With an injury as serious as this, it was always touch and go. Ben turned his attention back to the young man, feeling his concern deepen when he glanced at the monitor.

'BP's dropping,' Adam told him, his eyes scanning the lines and numbers that formed a visual record of their fight to save the patient's life.

'He's lost a lot of blood,' Ben said flatly. 'Get on to the lab and see how long it's going to be before they cross-match it. It needs to be done before he goes up to Theatre if he's to stand any chance at all.'

'I'll set up a chest drain.'

Zoë's voice, so cool, so calm, cut in then and he glanced at her. She looked perfectly composed and he was relieved to see that she no longer looked annoyed at the way he had summarily taken over. Maybe he should have allowed her to carry on but—hell!—she was pregnant and had recently undergone surgery. No one in his right mind would have allowed her to start lifting a patient in those circumstances.

'Fine,' Ben agreed, feeling a little better now that he had salved his conscience. 'I daren't remove the knife. It's the only thing that's stopping him bleeding out, so you'll have to work around it. You should be able to tell from the X-ray where to make the incision.'

'It isn't a problem,' she told him, swabbing an area on Ryan's side where she planned to make the incision.

Ben watched her cut through the flesh and underlying tissue with a steady hand. The intercostal muscle—the sheets of muscle between the ribs which helped expand and contract the chest during breathing—was tough but she zipped through it without any difficulty. Her actions were deft and sure and he was impressed. Zoë had honed her skills while she'd been in Paris and had turned into a fine doctor.

'The police are outside. They're going to contact Ryan's parents and the head of the college as well.'

'Good.' Jo came back and Ben returned his attention to what he was doing. It shouldn't have strayed in the first place but he was only human and having Zoë there, working alongside him, was bound to affect him.

Knowing that put him on his mettle. Using every skill he possessed, he fought to keep the young man alive. When Ryan's heart suddenly stopped beating, it was Ben who began to resuscitate him, Ben who decided which drugs were needed and Ben who applied the paddles of the defibrillator to Ryan's chest. It was a relief when the monitor once again showed a steady rhythm, the blips running in an orderly sequence across the screen. Although the knife was still *in situ*, Ryan was alive and had a better chance of staying that way as he was wheeled to Theatre. As the doors slapped shut behind the departing trolley, everyone broke into a round of applause and Ben grinned when he discovered the ovation was for him.

'Thank you kindly, folks. I'd offer to do an encore but I don't think we could go through a repeat at this moment.' He looked down at his bloodied apron and the pool of blood around his feet, and grimaced. 'Any more blood and guts in here and we'll be awash!'

Everyone laughed as they began to clear up. Jason summoned the cleaning team, who grumbled loudly when they saw the mess. Ben binned his apron and gloves then dipped his feet into a bucket of disinfectant to clean the soles of his shoes before he tramped through the department. The nursing staff all wore rubber-soled clogs but Zoë was wearing a smart pair of leather shoes. He smiled sympathetically when she gingerly dipped each foot into the water.

'Sorry about your footwear. Hazard of the job. I keep meaning to buy myself a pair of those rubber-soled thingummies but I never seem to get round to it. I must put it on my "to do" list.'

'They're very handy,' she agreed, using a wad of paper towels to dry her shoes. 'They're also the height of fashion so you will be very trendy if you do get round to buying yourself a pair.'

Ben chuckled as he elbowed his way out of Resus. 'I'm glad

you took this job. Not only are you proving to be a superb doctor, but you can give us all fashion tips!'

She laughed, her pretty face lighting up in a way that made his heart surge. She looked like the Zoë of old, he realised, then realised a second later just how much recent events had taken out of her. She was still incredibly beautiful but there was no denying that she looked very fragile and no wonder either. Who wouldn't be showing the effects of what she must be going through?

The urge to give her a hug was very strong. Ben's hands clenched because it was the last thing she would want him to do. While they were at work, she expected him to treat her the same as he treated everyone else, but it was going to be hard—very hard—once her pregnancy and the effects of her chemotherapy kicked in.

The thought of how he was going to manage to restrain his natural inclinations to protect her gave him hot and cold chills. Ben hid them the best way he could, smiling at her as though he hadn't a care in the world. 'I think we've earned a break, don't you? Come on, I'll treat you to a decent cup of coffee instead of that disgusting brew on offer in the staff room. Dalverston General has taken a major step into the modern world. We now have a café in the foyer that serves lattes!'

'Oh, wow! That's an offer I can't refuse.' She followed him through the waiting area and along the corridor that led to the front of the building. The newly built atrium looked particularly stunning with the sun shining through the glass roof and she stopped to admire it. 'It's really lovely. I had no idea that so much work had been done to the place. It must have cost a fortune.'

'It did, and they're still building.' Ben stopped and pointed out of the window. 'They're going to start knocking down the old bit of the hospital next month. The plan is to build a new radiology unit on the site—new scanners as well as X-ray equipment. Although we've had a CT scanner for ages, we've had to send patients to Manchester for an MRI scan, but that is about to change.'

'That's wonderful.'

Zoë leant forward so she could see better and Ben sucked in his breath when he felt her shoulder brush against his. However, it did little to control the fizz of excitement that coursed through his veins. It had always been the same: the moment Zoë had touched him he'd gone off with a bang and he was doing it again. Big time.

'So what do you fancy?' he asked, feeling deeply ashamed of himself. Zoë was pregnant *and* facing weeks of gruelling treatment, and here he was thinking about his physical needs! 'They have lattes, skinny lattes, moccachinos, cappuccinos, espresso…'

'Stop!' Zoë held up her hand, her grey eyes dancing with laughter. 'There's just too much choice. You choose for me and then it will be a nice surprise.'

'Sure? I might choose something you hate.'

'You know what I like, Ben. I trust you.'

'Do you?'

The question came out before he could stop it. Ben knew he shouldn't have asked her that, well, not in that tone at any rate. He looked into her eyes, oblivious to the fact that they were standing in the entrance to the café and that there were people milling around them. He didn't see them, didn't see anything except Zoë. He knew it was pointless even to think about it, but it would mean an awful lot to him if at least he had her trust.

'Do you trust me, Zoë? Do you know in your heart that I shall do my very best to help you?'

There was a moment when she didn't speak, when she just looked at him with sadness in her eyes before her head lowered.

Ben leant forward, afraid that he wouldn't hear her reply but, oddly, her voice was surprisingly strong when she spoke.

'Yes, I trust you, Ben. I would never have asked you to take care of our baby if anything happens to me if I didn't trust you.'

CHAPTER SEVEN

ZOË knew that her answer was only partly true but she was afraid to say anything more. She couldn't tell Ben the whole truth, that she trusted him more than she had ever trusted anyone else, when it would make her so vulnerable. When he excused himself to fetch their drinks, she breathed a sigh of relief. She wasn't sure if she could have held out if he'd pressed her.

She found them a table, watching the flow of people as they came and went. The café was popular with staff as well as visitors, although, surprisingly, she didn't recognise anyone in there that day. Ben had told her that there'd been a lot of staff changes recently and obviously it was true.

She sighed because why wouldn't it be true? Ben wouldn't have lied to her. He had always been completely honest with her. If he'd told her he'd been working late that was what he'd been doing, and if he'd arranged to meet her, he had never let her down. So why had she found it so hard to believe him when he'd told her that he would always love her?

Zoë felt her heart begin to race. All of a sudden she could see how foolish she'd been. Ben had told her the truth about that too and she hadn't believed him. She understood why, of course—she'd been afraid. Afraid that she would have her heart broken when he left her as everyone else had done. But Ben was different: he would never have left her. He wouldn't have stopped loving her either when he had given her his word. She'd been the one at fault. She hadn't trusted him to keep his promise despite the fact that he had never once let her down.

'I got you a latte in the end. I thought it best to play safe. I also got you a cherry slice, although you don't have to eat it if you don't want to.'

Ben put the tray on the table. Zoë felt her heart shrivel up as she realised how stupid she'd been. She and Ben could have spent the past two years together and they would have been happy too. It wouldn't have made any difference to the fact that she would still have had cancer, but then she could have turned to him without a qualm and let him help her. If there'd been a baby as well, they would have shared the joy and the fear for its future after her diagnosis, and it would have been so much easier because they would have done it together.

Now it was too late to get back what she'd lost. Ben may still be willing to help her, but she knew that his concern was for their child rather than for her. Oh, she didn't doubt that he was sorry she was ill, but all he probably felt for her now was sympathy, and who could blame him? When she had rejected his love two years ago, she had hurt him so much, destroyed any feelings he'd had for her. Although that night they had spent together had been a magical experience for her, she doubted if it had been the same for Ben when he had seen it as a way to finalise their relationship.

Even if she'd thought there was a chance that he still cared about her, it wouldn't be fair to act upon it, knowing that one day she might break his heart all over again if she died. She really couldn't do that to him. She would protect him just as fiercely as she would protect their unborn child.

* * *

Ben arranged the cups on the table and sat down. Zoë hadn't uttered a word, although he sensed it wasn't his choice of coffee that had caused her silence. He frowned when he saw the sadness on her face. Whatever was going through her mind, it wasn't anything cheerful.

'It was a bit hairy this morning, wasn't it? We don't see that many knifings in Dalverston, thankfully enough.' He summoned a smile when he saw that he had her attention. She had so many weighty issues to contend with that his heart quailed at the thought of what she must be going through, but if he could help her even a little bit by remaining up-beat, that's what he would do. 'They tend to happen more often in the cities—Manchester, Liverpool, London—Paris even?'

'We certainly saw our share in Paris,' she replied, and Ben breathed a little easier when he realised that he had successfully distracted her.

'Really? It's obviously a global problem. Mind you, although we don't deal with many knifings, we do see a lot more cases of drunkenness. Binge drinking is rife in the town and the consequences can be quite horrific at times too.'

He took a sip of his coffee, hiding his shudder. He hated lattes and couldn't think why he'd bought it. He grimaced. Oh, yes, he could. He'd been more concerned about what to get for Zoë than what he had wanted himself.

'It was the same where I worked. So many youngsters set out to get themselves drunk and end up in a real state. It doesn't make any sense to me.'

'Me neither. I guess it's an age thing.' He cupped his ear, grinning when she looked at him in surprise. 'I thought I heard someone muttering about the younger generation. It can't have been me. I'm way too young!'

'Oh, yes?' Zoë retorted. 'Correct me if I'm wrong but didn't you just celebrate another birthday? Was there enough room on the cake for all the candles?'

'Ouch! You know how to hit a guy where it hurts.' He clutched his heart, feigning anguish, then realised how easy it was to turn in a sterling performance. His heart did ache, although not because of his age. Knowing what Zoë was going through hurt unbearably.

There was no way he would admit that so he hammed it up for all he was worth. 'I'll have you know that I'm in my prime so you can stop casting aspersions, Dr Frost.'

'In your prime? Really? I would class thirty-five as being middle-aged.'

'Middle-aged,' he spluttered, not having to feign indignation this time.

'Mmm. The old three-score-and-ten remit. If you halve it, it makes thirty-five, ergo middle-age.'

She was the picture of innocence as she sat there sipping her coffee. Ben shook his head at being so cleverly outmanoeuvred. 'Well, I don't feel middle-aged. In fact, there's very little I can't do now that I could do when I was sixteen.'

'How about skateboarding?' she asked sweetly.

'Skateboarding?'

'Yes. Surely you remember that time we were in the park and you begged that kid to let you have a go on his skateboard. What was it you told him?' She pretended to think for a second, her eyes gleaming with laughter as she continued. 'Ah, yes, that you were junior champion when you were at school, although I must say that you looked a bit rusty to me.'

'Oh, that was below the belt! Just because I experienced a bit of difficulty getting back into the rhythm…'

'A *bit* of difficulty!' Her silky brows arched. 'You ended up with two cut knees and a badly bruised elbow, Ben. Oh, and you also had a massive bruise on your—'

'OK, OK!' Ben held up his hand, not wanting to be reminded of his badly bruised backside as well. He hadn't been able to sit down properly for over a week and didn't relish reliving that humiliating episode. 'Maybe I did exaggerate my prowess just a little.'

Zoë hooted with laughter. 'Exaggerated it a lot, you mean. You were hopeless!'

'All right, so it was a daft thing to do. Can I help it if I wanted to impress you?'

'Impress me?'

'Yep. I thought you'd be so bowled over when you saw me whizzing along like poetry in motion, you'd be putty in my hands.' He laughed, deliberately turning it into a joke although every word was true. He had wanted to impress her and he had failed miserably for his sins.

'You crafty devil! I'm glad you made a pig's ear of it now. It serves you right.'

She smiled at him, the warmth in her eyes making him feel all tingly inside. It was as though all the bad times had disappeared and they were back to how they'd been at the beginning, two people on the brink of falling in love...

Ben picked up his cup, forcing down a glug of the milky coffee. They couldn't go back and he wouldn't want to even if they could. It had been too painful and he didn't intend to repeat his mistakes. They had to look to the future, although heaven alone knew what the future held in store.

All of a sudden the fear he had tried so hard to keep in check all day reared its ugly head and he knew that he had to get away before Zoë realised how he felt. He stood up abruptly, forcing himself to smile when he saw her look at him in surprise.

'I've just remembered that I need to phone the office to confirm you started today. If I don't do it now, I might not get another opportunity. You stay and enjoy your coffee. There's no need to rush back.'

He didn't wait for her to reply, didn't want to know if she had seen through the lie. Although he did need to contact the office, it could have waited. He made his way to the lift, deciding that he may as well hand over the information in person. It would give him breathing space, time to get back on track.

He sighed as he stepped into the lift. Would he ever get back on course again, though? Having Zoë here was already having an effect on him and it would continue to do so throughout the coming months. They hadn't discussed what would happen after the baby was born, but there was no way that she was going back to Paris. He refused to be shut out of his child's life until he was needed.

His heart sank as the implications of that thought hit him. He would be needed if anything happened to Zoë, but he couldn't allow himself to wonder if her treatment would work. Their baby needed a father and a mother and, please, heaven, he or she would have both of them around for a very long time. Closing his eyes, Ben did something he hadn't done for ages— he prayed. He didn't pray for himself—that would have been a waste. Every prayer needed to be directed to the woman he had once loved more than life itself, and their precious child. He wanted them both to be safe.

It was a long day and Zoë was exhausted by the time they got back to the apartment. Ben had moved out of the flat they had shared into a new apartment overlooking the river. It was bright and airy, with pale wooden floors, oodles of white paint and gadgets galore, but she preferred the old place. The apartment might be beautiful, but it had no soul. It looked like somewhere Ben came to sleep, but it didn't look like his home.

The thought nagged at her as she followed him into the sitting room. Apart from the cardboard boxes that she'd stacked up in one corner, the room was immaculate. There were no magazines lying on the chrome-and-glass coffee-tables, no knick-knacks, nothing personal belonging to Ben. It looked like a room featured in a glossy magazine and it worried her to see the way he had been living.

'How long have you lived here?' she asked as Ben slumped down onto one of the black leather sofas.

'Almost two years. I bought it soon after you left for Paris,' he told her, picking up the remote control to switch on the plasma screen television. It came zooming up out of its hiding place, an all-singing, all-dancing media unit in stainless steel that Zoë had hated on sight, and she frowned. Ben had liked old furniture in the past, items that were full of character, so what had brought about such a massive change in his taste? And what had happened to the things they had bought together at various flea-markets and antique shops?

'What did you do with all our old furniture?' she demanded, not giving herself time to consider the wisdom of what she was doing.

'I got rid of it.' He switched on the news, lowering the sound as he looked at her. 'One of the nurses needed some stuff so I gave most of it to her and I sold the rest on the internet.'

'Why?' She sat down on one of the matching black leather armchairs, not that it had arms, just three sides all the same height. It was the sort of chair she loathed, difficult to get comfortable in and even more difficult to get out of, and she wished with all her heart that Ben had kept the lumpy old armchair that had been her favourite place to curl up after a busy day.

'Because it wasn't needed.' He swept a hand round the room. 'This was the show flat and it came with all the furniture included. There wouldn't have been room for the other stuff even if it had suited this place, which it wouldn't have done.'

'I see.' Zoë did see, saw a lot more than he was admitting, in fact. Had Ben decided to make a clean sweep, get rid of everything so he wouldn't have any reminders of their life together?

She guessed it was true and it grieved her to know how much she must have hurt him if he'd preferred to rid himself of any trace of her presence. Standing up, she headed for the kitchen because there was no way she could apologise or make things right. She had to remain emotionally detached if she was to get through the next few months. 'I'll make a start on dinner. I take it there's food in the fridge.'

'I stocked up at the weekend, but I'll cook, Zoë. You sit down and relax.'

'I'm not an invalid, Ben.' She waved him back to his seat, hurting inside and angry with herself because she couldn't afford to feel this way. 'I am perfectly capable of cooking us a meal.'

'Fine. It's up to you.'

Ben sank back onto the sofa, turning up the volume so he could listen to the news. Zoë didn't say a word as she went and hung her coat in the hall closet. Like everything else in the apartment, it was state of the art: she pressed a button, the door opened and the light came on, and she hated it too. She much preferred the old coat rack they'd had, the one with the wobbly leg and what Ben had claimed was woodworm, although she had always disagreed with him. As she'd pointed out on many occasions, she had never, ever seen a worm climbing up the coat rack!

Zoë smiled wistfully as she closed the closet door. It was an old joke and one they had enjoyed many times in the past too.

They'd had a lot of fun together, shared the ups and downs of daily life until Ben had wanted to make it permanent. Would she have left if he hadn't suggested marriage? she wondered as she opened the chiller side of the glass-and-stainless-steel refrigeration unit—nothing this spectacular could be called a fridge!

Probably not, she conceded, taking out a couple of lamb chops and some tiny new potatoes. She had been terrified by the thought of making a legal commitment, yet they'd been committed to each other, hadn't they? They hadn't needed a marriage licence to be truly a couple—they'd been that anyway. And yet the moment Ben had mentioned marriage and the future, she'd taken flight. How stupid she'd been to run away from something so good.

A tear trickled down her cheek and she dashed it away. She had dinner to prepare and prepare it she would. It was the least she could do for Ben in return for his kindness and the love he had once showered on her.

Ben paused in the kitchen doorway, feeling his heart contract when he saw the tear slide down Zoë's cheek. He felt like crying too, crying for the way she was suffering, for her fear as well as the fear he felt for her, but it wouldn't be fair. Zoë had enough to cope with without him going to pieces. Taking a deep breath, he went into the kitchen.

'I'll set the table. Do you want to eat in here or in the dining room?'

'Here's fine by me, but you choose.'

'We'll eat in here then.'

He laid two places for them, smoothing out the linen mats and lining up the cutlery with military precision. Zoë was grilling the lamb chops and he looked round when he heard the smoke alarm start beeping.

'Damn!' She swore softly as she flapped a tea-towel beneath the alarm. 'This thing is really sensitive.'

'It is. You need to use the extractor fan when you're cooking.' Leaning past her, he flicked a switch and the fan whirred into action, sucking up the smoke in a trice. 'There you go.'

'Thanks.' She turned the chops over, casting a wary eye ceilingward in case the spitting fat set off another ear-splitting blast.

'You should be safe enough now. The extractor is pretty efficient. It should be able to cope with your cooking, not to mention your toast making. That will be the ultimate test, of course.'

'Cheek!'

She cast him a baleful look and he grinned at her, wanting to enjoy these moments while they could. A time might come when they couldn't find much to joke about and he wanted to store up the good times in readiness for then.

'It's true, Zoë. Every single morning when you made toast our old smoke alarm used to get its daily workout. We got through more batteries than I could count!'

'I like my toast well done,' she told him huffily.

'There's well done and there's *well done*,' he retorted. 'Toast used to be served in varying degrees of blackness ranging from charcoal to cremation.'

'You never complained,' she pointed out. 'You were happy enough to eat it no matter what colour it was. So long as you didn't have to get up first and make breakfast, you didn't care.'

'True.' He held up his hands in defeat. 'You've got me there. When it comes to getting up of a morning, I need a cup of coffee before I can function properly.'

Zoë laughed. 'Heaven only knows how you've managed since I left.' She broke off and he saw the colour rush to her cheeks. 'Sorry. I'm assuming an awful lot, aren't I?'

'That there's been no one else around to burn my toast?' He

shrugged, knowing that he couldn't lie to her. 'You assume correctly. I haven't lived with anyone else, although I can't claim to have been celibate these past two years.'

'Oh. Right. Well, that's your business, of course.'

She picked up the pan of potatoes and went to the sink to drain off the water. Ben saw her wince when some of the hot water splashed the back of her hand.

'Here, use the lid. It's got drainage holes in it.' He offered her the lid but she didn't appear to see it and his heart sank when he saw the tears that were trickling down her face. Had she scalded herself that badly?

He took the pan from her and turned her round while he checked her hands. They looked all right to him but she was still crying silently, as though she hated the fact that she was showing any sign of emotion. Did she really think she had to present a brave face all the time? he wondered sadly. Didn't she know that he understood how scared she must feel?

He drew her into his arms, hoping that in some small way he could provide the comfort she needed. Maybe they weren't going to share their lives again as they had done before, but he could share this with her, share her pain and her fear. Zoë might believe that she needed his help only for the sake of their baby, but he knew differently. At the present moment *she* needed him too!

The thought was just too poignant. Ben didn't pause to think as he bent and kissed her. He knew that Zoë wouldn't listen if he tried to explain that he wanted to be there for her so he would show her through actions rather than words that he cared. It seemed to work because she immediately responded, kissing him back with a hunger that bordered on desperation.

Ben lifted her into his arms when he felt her body press against his in a way he recognised only too well. It took him just a few moments to carry her into his bedroom and lay her down on the bed but even that was too long. This may have started with him wanting to comfort her but all of a sudden he needed comforting too. He needed to be close to her and for a few precious moments know that she was safe in his arms.

He stripped off her clothes and stripped off his own, letting them fall on the floor. Zoë's eyes were closed but her arms reached up and enfolded him when he went back to her. There was no hesitation as she pulled him down to her, no reason for him to doubt what they were doing. It wasn't a case of it being right or wrong but necessary. Zoë needed him to allay her fears and, by heaven, that's what he intended to do!

Ben kissed the scar on her left breast and felt her shudder. At any other time he knew she would have felt embarrassed about her recent surgery, but her need was too great for feelings like that to intrude now. Ben certainly wasn't put off by what he saw, although he did grieve for what had once been perfect and wasn't as perfect any more. Her breast would never look the same again, but in his heart he knew it didn't matter. He was just grateful that Zoë had been given a chance to beat this terrible illness.

He kissed her there again, then kissed her other breast and her mouth, and then there was no way he could hold back any longer. He needed to be inside her, give her the comfort they both needed so desperately. Their love-making was more intense than anything he had experienced. Conscious of the baby in her womb, he made love to her with a gentleness he hadn't believed himself capable of before. It was love-making in its purest form, a joining of their souls as well as their bodies.

That night they scaled new heights together and as they came back to earth some time later, Ben knew that it would take very little to fall in love with her again, only he couldn't risk it. He couldn't deal with the fear of having his heart broken on top of everything else. He would do everything in his power to help her and their child but he wouldn't let himself love her: he couldn't.

CHAPTER EIGHT

'I KNOW how daunting this must seem to you, Zoë. However, I'm confident that we can get you and your baby safely through the next few months.'

'Thank you.'

Zoë returned the other woman's smile, hoping her nervousness didn't show. It was Monday morning and she had her first appointment with Deborah Gaston, the oncology consultant. Daniel Walker, the obstetrician in charge of her care, had asked if he could sit in so he was there as well. That made four of them in the office including her and Ben.

Zoë took a quick little breath as Ben leant forward and picked up the notes Deborah had prepared for them. There hadn't been a repeat of what had happened the other evening—she'd made sure of that. Although she didn't regret making love with Ben, it would be wrong to let it happen again. It wasn't fair to use him as an emotional crutch when the future was so uncertain. At the moment, she couldn't see beyond the next few months, beyond getting through her chemo and giving birth to their baby.

'I've been in touch with several consultants who have experience of this type of situation and they were all very encouraging. Following their advice, I intend to adjust the drugs you'll be given. Instead of the usual regime of FEC—that's fluorouracil, epirubicin and cyclophosphamide—which is the gold standard for treating breast cancer, I shall drop the florouracil and give you a double dose of cyclophosphamide.'

Deborah looked at her and Zoë nodded, determined that she was going to stick to her decision. She would keep Ben on the periphery of her life as much as it was possible to do so. 'You're the expert, Miss Gaston. I'll abide by whatever you decide.'

'Good. From what I've been told that's the best way forward.' Deborah turned to Daniel. 'Are you happy with that, Daniel?'

'As Zoë said, you're the expert, Deborah. I'm more than happy to leave that side of things to you.' Daniel turned to Zoë and she saw the compassion in his eyes as he looked from her to Ben. 'I know how worrying this must be for you both, but I'm confident that we shall deliver a healthy baby at the end of it. We'll scan you every two weeks throughout your pregnancy and it goes without saying that if you have any problems, we shall deal with them immediately.'

'There's still a risk to the child, though,' Ben said quietly.

Zoë's heart ached when she heard the strain in his voice. Maybe no one else in the room could hear it but she knew him too well. Reaching out, she gripped his hand even though she had sworn that she wouldn't cross the dividing line again. She had to stay on one side and Ben on the other, each of them dealing with any emotional issues the best way they could. They'd needed each other the other night and it had helped, too, but they couldn't handle this as a couple when it could make it all the more difficult for him in the future, alone. She gently withdrew her hand, because it wasn't fair to Ben to pick and choose when she offered him her support.

'The drugs could adversely affect the baby,' he stated bluntly.

'They could. However, the fact that chemo will be starting

at sixteen weeks, when the foetus is fully formed, means that their effect should be minimal.'

Daniel sounded full of confidence and Zoë saw Ben relax and felt a little better. Maybe she did need to maintain her distance but she couldn't pretend that it didn't hurt to see him suffering. They left the office a short time later, armed with the notes Deborah had prepared for them. Ben sighed as he tucked them under his arm.

'Looks like we have some reading to do tonight.'

'I'm on a late, don't forget,' Zoë reminded him, pressing the button to summon the lift.

'Drat! I'd forgotten about that.' Ben followed her into the lift, frowning as he watched her select the ground floor. 'Do you think it's a good idea to carry on working while you're having your treatment, Zoë? It's bound to knock you sideways and with you being pregnant as well…' He trailed off and shrugged.

'I don't have much option. I need to earn a living,' Zoë said shortly because it was something she had thought about a lot. She had no idea how the chemotherapy was going to affect her and it was worrying to think that she might feel too ill to work.

'That's crazy! You know very well that you don't need to work. I'm more than happy to support you.'

'Yes, I do know that, but it wouldn't be fair, Ben.' She shook her head when he went to interrupt her. 'I'm sorry but I've made up my mind and you're not going to change it. I have no intention of freeloading off you.'

'And I have no intention of standing back while you wear yourself out,' he retorted. The lift had reached the ground floor but he ignored the fact that the doors had opened. 'You need to see some sense.'

'No, what you mean is that I need to fall in with your views. Don't try to ride roughshod over me, Ben, because I won't have it, do you hear?'

She stalked out of the lift, angry with him for trying to take over her life this way. At the moment all she had was her job—it was the only thing that made her life feel normal. And she didn't intend to give it up until she absolutely had to do so.

'Is it just the money or the fact that you don't want to be beholden to me?'

Ben followed her along the corridor, his long legs quickly closing the gap between them. Zoë cast him a baleful look, wishing he would accept what she said without asking all these questions. It was her decision to carry on working, just as it had been her decision to have this baby, although she might not have been so sure about what she was doing if he hadn't agreed to help her, as she had known he would do.

All the fight drained out of her as she was forced to admit that she had taken his agreement for granted right from the outset. Oh, she'd felt nervous about asking him for help, but deep down she had known he wouldn't refuse. She should be glad that Ben was who he was, someone who would never shirk his responsibilities.

'Probably both of those things,' she admitted. 'Although they're not the only reasons. I need to carry on working for my sake too. It's the only thing that makes my life seem normal at the moment. I also believe it will help if I have something else to focus on when I'm having a bad day.'

'When the chemo kicks in?'

'Yes. Or if I'm suddenly struck down by an attack of morning sickness.'

She dredged up a smile, not wanting the mood to become too downbeat. Ben grinned back at her, although she could tell that it was an effort for him to appear so cheery. Trust Ben to play his part, she thought. It was typical of him to put her needs first and his own second.

'You may have escaped that bit. Isn't it more usual to suffer morning sickness in the first three months? My sister Katie was terrible when she had her youngest. She threw up every morning until she hit the three-month mark and it stopped like magic. With a bit of luck, you've bypassed the yucky stage.'

'I hope you're right. Mind you, I'll probably make up for it by developing cravings.' Her smile was less forced, the sensation of warmth that filled her making her feel much better. Ben may not be in love with her any more but he obviously cared about her. Knowing that helped her feel more positive.

'Start eating coal or snacking on pickles and jam, you mean?'

He laughed out loud, a rich deep sound that made Zoë's skin tingle with awareness. She'd always loved his laugh, always found it deeply sexy, and in that respect nothing had changed. The only difference was that now she couldn't allow herself to respond to it the way she'd done in the past. And Ben wouldn't want her to either.

'It sounds as though I'll have to keep an eye on you, Zoë, and make sure you stick to a more conventional diet. Just let me know if you start fancying anything strange, will you?'

'I shall.' She paused as they reached the foyer, glad of an excuse to put some distance between them. The problem with being around Ben was that it made her want to be with him all the time and that wouldn't do. 'I'll be off, then. Have a good day. I'll see you at lunchtime, I expect.'

Ben shook his head. 'I doubt it. I've a meeting in Leeds this afternoon so I'm driving over there at noon. A working party on trauma care,' he added by way of explanation. 'Don't be surprised if I'm not back when you get home tonight. We usually have dinner afterwards. It's the perfect opportunity to have a good moan about the state of the NHS.'

'Oh, right. I won't wait up, then. Have fun.'

Zoë gave him a quick smile then hurried out of the door. It was a blustery March day, the clouds scudding across a milky-blue sky. There was still a sprinkling of snow on the tops of the hills but the weather was definitely warming up as spring approached. She had been planning on going into town to do some shopping, wary of leaving everything to the last minute to prepare for the baby in case she wasn't well enough to do it then. However, the thought of trailing around the shops no longer appealed. She would go back to the apartment and have a couple of hours to herself before she came back to work.

She sighed as she headed to the bus stop. From the sound of it she would have more than a couple of hours to herself today. Obviously, Ben was looking forward to meeting up with his colleagues from the working party. Dinner and some interesting conversation must be preferable to spending an evening at home, waiting for her to get back from work.

She pulled herself up short. Ben was free to come and go as he pleased. He certainly didn't need to factor her into his plans!

The meeting dragged on. Normally, Ben enjoyed the opportunity to exchange views with like-minded people, but that day he just wanted to get it over. They seemed to be going over and over old ground, with no decisions being made. When the chairman asked for a show of hands on the latest proposal, he gnashed his teeth in frustration. Six for and six against—hell! That meant another round of discussions.

It was gone six before the meeting finally broke up. Most of the group was going on to a local restaurant but Ben refused when he was asked to join them. He knew it was silly but he didn't like to think of Zoë going home to an empty apartment after her shift.

He drove back to Dalverston, thinking about what had

happened that morning. Deborah had sounded very encouraging but, then, she would take that approach—he would have done the same himself. Having a positive mental attitude wouldn't cure an illness but it helped the patient when it came to coping with any side effects. If he could keep Zoë feeling positive, it might help her too.

He sighed as he pulled out to overtake a lorry that was blocking the middle lane. He would need to do a better job than he'd done that morning if he was to achieve that objective. It was Zoë who had squeezed *his* hand and tried to reassure *him*. He'd definitely had a wobble but it would be the last time. When he was with Zoë he was going to make sure he oozed confidence even if it killed him!

The thought had barely crossed his mind when the lorry he was overtaking veered sideways. Ben had just a split second to react and slammed his foot on the brake. There was an ear-scorching crunch of metal as the lorry collided with his car, catapulting him into the central crash barrier. The ensuing jolt made his teeth snap together but when the car came to a halt he was still breathing and didn't appear to be injured in any way. The lorry had stopped several yards ahead, slewed across the carriageway. Ben held his breath as he waited for the ensuing carnage but, amazingly, everyone managed to stop in time. By the time he got out to see if he could help, traffic was at a standstill.

'I'm a doctor,' he explained, pushing his way through the crowd that was gathering around the lorry. It was a foreign vehicle and the driver was seated on the left of the cab instead of on the right. Ben climbed up the steps, taking in the scene at a glance. The driver was slumped sideways and appeared to be unconscious. He obviously hadn't been wearing a seat belt either.

Wrenching open the door, Ben leant into the cab and felt for a pulse, relieved when he found one even though it was extremely fast and thready. Climbing inside the cab, he listened to the man's breathing and was alarmed when he realised how laboured it sounded. If the driver hadn't been wearing a seat belt, he had probably hit the steering-wheel with some force, causing severe injuries to his chest which would account for his difficulty in breathing. It was a situation Ben had seen many times before and one he knew needed urgent attention.

Jumping down from the cab, he took out his mobile phone and called 999. An ambulance had already been dispatched, he was informed, so he asked the operator to tell the crew that the lorry driver had suffered suspected crush injuries to his chest. It would help speed things up if they knew what they were dealing with before they got there.

By the time everything was sorted out, it was gone eight o'clock. Ben's car was a write-off so he begged a lift with the paramedics seeing as the ambulance was going to Dalverston General. It was lucky he did so because the lorry driver arrested on the way there. Ben did what he could—cardiac massage, a shot of adrenaline followed by a couple of rounds with the defibrillator—and managed to stabilise him, but it was touch and go. It was a relief when they reached the hospital.

He ran alongside the trolley as the crew rushed it through to Resus. Jo was on duty that night and Jason too, and they both looked at him in surprise as he crashed through the doors. 'Don't ask,' he said with a shake of his head. 'Let's just say that I was in the wrong place at the wrong time.'

'Or the right place at the right time if you're this chap,' Jo replied, grabbing a corner of the spinal board.

Ben grinned at her. 'I'll take that as a compliment, shall I?'

'You may as well. You look as if you could do with a bit of a boost. Have you seen the state of yourself?'

Ben glanced down and only then realised that he was looking decidedly the worse for wear. The knee of one trouser leg was sporting a large hole and there was blood on his shirt too. Raising his hand, he gingerly felt his nose and grimaced. 'Ouch! I must have bumped my nose when the lorry hit me.'

'No sense, no feeling,' Jo muttered, whizzing a pair of scissors up the driver's jacket sleeve.

The doors flipped open before Ben could reply and he glanced round, feeling a smile start to form when he saw Zoë. Maybe it was only a few hours since he'd seen her, but he couldn't pretend that he hadn't missed her, he thought, then wondered why. The days when spending time apart from Zoë had been pure torture should have been well past.

'Hi,' he said, getting a grip on himself because the accident must have shaken him up more than he'd realised. 'I didn't think I'd end up in here again today,' he began then paused when he saw her eyes widen. 'Zoë? Are you OK? What's wrong?'

'I… You…. Oh!'

Her face turned a sickly shade of white. Ben took a hasty step forward then stopped when someone appeared behind her. It was Sam Kearney, senior registrar of Dalverston's A & E and he was carrying a child in his arms.

'Let's get her on the bed, Zoë,' Sam said tersely.

Zoë made an obvious effort to collect herself as she followed Sam to the bed. Ben knew he couldn't spare the time to check that she was all right, but it wasn't easy to ignore her as he turned back to the lorry driver. 'We need X-rays,' he said because it was the first thing that came to mind.

'We're way ahead of you, boss,' Jo said cheerily as the radiographer manoeuvred the equipment overhead. Everyone moved out of the way while the X-rays were taken and then it was back to business—Jo finished cutting off the patient's clothing, Jason put in a second line and Claire Jones, their very new house officer, flitted back and forth, looking flustered.

'Slow down,' Ben told her, trying to blot out what was happening across the room. He could hear Zoë's voice in the background and had to struggle to keep himself focussed. She had looked so shocked when she'd seen him and he longed to reassure her that he was all right...

He made himself stop there. There was no point imagining how he would have taken her in his arms and held her close so she would have known for certain that he wasn't injured. Fat chance of him doing that in the middle of Resus with all the staff watching—they'd have had a field day! And even fatter chance of Zoë letting him.

'Mistakes happen when folk try to rush,' he told Claire firmly, blanking out that pertinent thought. 'You need to work speedily but always remain in control of the situation. Take a few seconds to assess the pros and cons of your actions. That way there'll be less chance of something unforeseen happening.'

'Sorry. It's just all so new and scary.'

Claire bit her lip and Ben could tell that she was overcome by the drama of what she was witnessing. It happened quite often to young doctors fresh out of medical school. The time they'd spent on the wards during their training didn't prepare them for the urgency of emergency care. Ben was determined it wasn't going to happen in this instance and nodded to the patient.

'I want you to monitor his BP very closely. Can you do that, Claire?'

'Of course!'

Claire beamed as she stepped closer to the bed and stared fixedly at the monitor. Jo caught his eye and winked, understanding what Ben was doing by giving the junior doctor the task. The monitoring equipment would soon tell them if there was a problem with the patient's blood pressure, but they both knew it would help Claire if she had something to concentrate on.

'X-rays are up,' the radiographer called and he went to take a look, frowning when he discovered that the patient's sternum was fractured in two places, at the manubrium—the top triangle-shaped portion—where it joined the body of the sternum, and close to the xiphoid process—the small leaf-shaped bit at the very bottom.

'No wonder he's having problems breathing,' he said, calling Claire over and pointing to the screen. 'The joint between the manubrium and the body of the sternum—it's called a symphysis joint,' he added for her benefit, 'has been damaged. That means there's reduced flexibility during breathing.'

'The heart may have been damaged if the sternum is broken,' Claire suggested tentatively.

'It could indeed. Well done for remembering that,' Ben praised her, pleased to see that she was getting into her stride. He pointed to the screen again. 'Fortunately that doesn't appear to have happened in this instance, although undoubtedly there's been severe bruising caused to the heart. In this type of accident the heart gets squashed between the sternum and the spine. It often ruptures, which is immediately fatal, of course. This chap's been lucky, but the severity of the bruising could be a major factor that determines his recovery. We'll finish stabilising him and leave it to the cardiac team to decide how to proceed.'

Claire went back to her post while Ben made a thorough check on their patient. There were no other major injuries apart from the ones he had noted so once the cardiac reg arrived, he handed over the driver.

Zoë was still working with Sam and he went across to see

if they needed a hand, trying to still the noisy beat of his heart when Zoë looked at him with worried grey eyes.

'Are you OK?' she said, and he nodded.

'Yep. I got caught up in an accident on the Motorway—the guy we've just sent to the cardio unit was driving the lorry that tried to demolish my car,' he explained, trying to make light of it. It didn't work because she blanched and he cursed himself for telling her too much.

'I'm fine,' he assured her. 'Take no notice of the state of my clothes—I must have bumped my nose and that accounts for the blood. It's certainly tender.'

He gingerly felt his nose, hoping to allay her fears. Zoë gave him a quick smile. 'You were lucky.'

'I was.' Ben felt his heart race when he saw the relief in her eyes. It was obvious that she had been worried about him and the thought made him want to punch the air for joy before it struck him that it didn't mean anything. She would probably have been equally concerned about any of their colleagues.

It was a depressing thought for some reason. Fortunately, Sam Kearney chipped in just then and Ben didn't have time to dwell on it.

'I wouldn't mind another opinion, Ben. Have a listen to this little one's chest, will you?' Sam glanced at the little girl. 'She was in a house fire—chip pan caught fire but Dad managed to put it out while Mum got the kids out of the house. The other two children are fine but this little lady is having problems with her oxygen levels. Her sats are way too low and we can't seem to get them up.'

Ben took the stethoscope Sam offered him and smiled at the little girl. 'Hi. I'm just going to listen to your chest, sweetheart. Is that OK?'

She nodded her head then lay perfectly still while he listened to her chest, back and front, and examined her throat. 'There's no sign of swelling to the tissues in the throat,' he observed, looking up.

'According to the mother, the children were in the front room and there was very little smoke in there,' Zoë explained.

Ben nodded, determined to stick to what was important at the moment, the child's well-being. He would worry about why he had felt so depressed at the thought of Zoë treating him the same as any other colleague later. 'So it's doubtful if the amount of smoke she inhaled has caused a problem with her breathing. Any history of asthma?'

'No. That was one of the first things we checked with the parents when she was admitted,' Zoë replied.

'In that case, I'd say it needs further investigation,' Ben concluded. 'Sorry I can't be more help.'

'Not to worry. We'll just have to try a different line of enquiry, won't we, Zoë?' Sam turned to Zoë, who shrugged.

'Looks like it. Hopefully, we'll learn more when the results of the bloods come back, although I'm pretty sure there's something else going on.'

'It sounds as though you've got everything covered,' Ben said lightly, handing back the stethoscope. 'In which case, I'll leave you to it. I'll see you later,' he added, glancing at Zoë, and was surprised when he saw her colour.

'Yes.' She didn't say anything else and Ben was left with the distinct impression that he'd said something wrong, although he had no idea what…

He groaned as he left Resus. Zoë probably hadn't wanted anyone to know that she was staying with him and now he'd let the cat out of the bag, although how she'd hoped to keep it a secret, he had no idea. Although personal data was supposed to be confidential, someone would have found out that they were living at the same address. Then there was the fact that they'd been seen together in the oncology unit that morning—people would soon know about that too.

He frowned. This was something they hadn't considered: what were they going to tell everyone about Zoë's illness and the baby? It all depended how much she wanted people to know. One thing was certain, though, they needed to present a united front if they hoped to avoid a lot of unsavoury gossip. People would think it was very strange when they discovered that he and Zoë were having a baby, yet weren't really a couple, so they would have to gloss over the facts.

His heart sank. He hated to think that he might have to lie to the people he worked with, yet it could come down to that. He was merely acting as a back-up in case things went wrong, but in no way did Zoë want to be with him on a permanent basis.

Pain speared through him and he grimaced. It still hurt to know how she felt and it was pointless denying it. He had loved her so much but she hadn't wanted him or his love. It was only in fairy-tales that the couple rode off into the sunset and lived happily ever after. Real life was far more complicated. Now all he wanted was to be allowed to help her and their baby. Maybe it wasn't much compared to what he had dreamed about once, but it was enough. He didn't intend to risk his heart all over again.

CHAPTER NINE

THE results of the blood tests arrived shortly before Zoë was due to leave work. Sam called her over and they went into the office to read them. Zoë's heart sank because, according to the data they'd received, little Bethany Morris had a worryingly high white-cell count. There were also blast cells—immature blood cells—present in her blood.

Sam shook his head. 'I don't like the look of this. If I had to lay odds on it, I'd bet that Bethany has leukaemia.'

'It certainly looks that way from these figures. It would also account for her low oxygen levels and fatigue, wouldn't it?' Zoë sighed. 'The white cells are invading her body and there's not enough red blood cells to carry oxygen from her lungs.'

'I wonder if the parents have noticed anything unusual. There are usually other symptoms—headaches, joint pains, tenderness, etcetera.'

'We'd better ask them. We'll also check if there's any sign of swelling in the lymph nodes. That would be a good indication that we're on the right track.'

'It would.' Sam grimaced. 'We were so sure that Bethany's symptoms were the result of smoke inhalation, we didn't explore any other options.' He glanced at his watch. 'You're due to finish soon, aren't you? I can deal with this if you want to get off.'

He didn't say it but Zoë knew he was remembering that comment Ben had made about seeing her later. Although she didn't want to advertise what was going on, she liked Sam and knew it would easier if he had some idea of the situation.

'Ben knows where I am.' She shrugged. 'I'm staying with him at the moment.'

'Easier than having to find a place of your own when you've just got back from France,' Sam replied evenly and she decided to leave it at that. She would tell him the rest if and when she needed to.

She sighed as they left the office. It wasn't a case of *if* but *when* surely? There was no way that she could hide her pregnancy and no way that she wouldn't start to show the effects of the chemotherapy either. At some point everyone would need to know and she had to decide what she was going to tell them.

It was worrying to wonder what people would think when they found out that she and Ben were having a baby, but she put it aside while they went to speak to Bethany's parents. Mr and Mrs Morris were sitting with their daughter in one of the cubicles and they both looked up when she and Sam went in.

'Sorry about the delay but we wanted to see the results of the blood tests,' Sam explained.

'She seems a bit better now, Doctor,' Alison Morris said hopefully.

'That's good.' Zoë smiled at the couple, wishing they didn't have to turn their world inside out. If she and Sam were correct in their suspicions, this would be just the start for the family and there would be far worse times to come.

The memory of her own shock at being told she had cancer helped her understand how distraught the parents were going to be. Zoë chose her words with care. 'Bethany's blood test results aren't quite what we expected. Can you tell us how she's been lately? Has she been her usual self or have you noticed any changes in her?'

'I'm not sure,' Alison said uncertainly. 'She's seemed a little more tired than normal, but I put that down to the fact that she had that tummy bug at Christmas. We all had it, in fact. It was awful!'

'There's been a lot of it around,' Sam said evenly. 'Apart from that, have you noticed anything else? Has Bethany complained that her legs ache, for instance, or does she seem to be getting a lot more bruises?'

'Why, yes!' Alison Morris exclaimed. 'Only this morning she started crying as we were walking to school, said that her legs hurt and she couldn't walk any further. It ended up with me carrying her.'

'And she did have a couple of nasty bruises on her shins last week,' Steve Morris put in. 'I noticed them when I was giving her a bath and asked her how she'd got them but she didn't know.' He glanced at his wife. 'She's also complained of having a headache a few times too.'

'That's right, she has.' Alison was looking really upset now. 'What's this all about, Doctor? Are you saying there's something seriously wrong with our Beth?'

'We think there's a possibility,' Zoë said quietly. 'However, Bethany will need to undergo some more tests before we can be sure.'

'Tests? What sort of tests?' Alison demanded, clutching Bethany's hand tightly.

'More blood tests and possibly a bone-marrow biopsy as well,' Sam explained gently.

'Bone marrow!' Steve blanched. 'They do that with those poor little kiddies who have leukaemia. Is that what you think is wrong with Beth?'

Both parents were becoming increasingly agitated and it

was upsetting Bethany. Zoë glanced pointedly towards the cubicle entrance and Sam nodded.

'Why don't we go to the relatives' room while we discuss this?' he suggested. 'You'll stay here with Bethany, won't you, Dr Frost?'

'Of course.' Zoë sat down beside the bed after the parents reluctantly allowed themselves to be ushered away. Picking up a book that one of the nurses had left on the trolley, she smiled at the little girl. 'Shall I read you a story until your mummy and daddy come back?'

She had just finished when Sam returned with the child's parents, who looked grey with worry. It was a relief when Sam quietly told her he could manage and that she was to go home. Zoë fetched her coat, deciding that she would take a taxi rather than wait for a bus. She hadn't realised how exhausting it would be to deal with such a highly emotive case and she felt completely drained. Ben was listening to some music when she let herself in and he turned down the sound when he heard her footsteps crossing the hall.

'Hi! You're late. Did you get held up?'

'Yes.' Zoë didn't bother to remove her coat as she sank down on the nearest seat. Tipping back her head, she closed her eyes as exhaustion washed over her. She heard Ben get up but couldn't muster enough energy to wonder what he was doing.

'Here you go. I made you some supper.' There was the rattle of cutlery as he placed a tray on a table and moved it closer to the chair. Zoë managed to prise one eyelid open a fraction and saw him smile at her. 'It's nothing much, just soup and a sandwich.'

'It's lovely. Thank you.'

Zoë felt her eyes well with tears as she looked at the tray. There was a steaming bowl of vegetable soup and a roast beef sandwich to go with it. There was even a napkin, only paper, but that didn't matter. It was the fact that Ben had taken the trouble to prepare it for her that counted.

'I know my cookery skills aren't exactly cordon bleu level but I don't usually reduce people to tears,' he teased her and she found herself smiling and sniffing at the same time. Picking up the spoon, he placed it in her hand. 'Go on, be brave and risk a mouthful.' His voice dropped to the level of a stage whisper. 'I didn't actually *make* it. I just opened the can.'

Zoë dipped the spoon into the bowl and scooped up a mouthful. 'It's delicious.'

'Phew!' He pretended to wipe sweat from his brow. 'Worth slaving over a hot can opener.'

He went back to his seat, leaving her to eat her supper in peace. Zoë felt a lump come to her throat and forced it down as she bit into the sandwich. She didn't deserve to be spoilt like this when she had done nothing to deserve it. She had caused him so much pain yet he treated her with such kindness. Would he have behaved this way if she hadn't been pregnant with his child? she wondered suddenly. She knew how Ben felt about children, that he adored them, and it could explain why he was so eager to lavish attention on her.

The thought took away some of her pleasure but she made herself finish every scrap of her supper for the baby's sake. 'That was lovely,' she said finally, pushing the tray aside. 'Thank you.'

'You're welcome. Do you want a coffee? Or tea, perhaps?' Ben half rose but she waved him back to his seat.

'No, I've had more than enough. It was really good of you to make it for me, but I don't expect you to wait on me, Ben.'

'I just thought you might need a bit of an energy boost. It's been an eventful day, one way and another.'

'It has.' Zoë bit her lip as she recalled the shock she'd had when she'd seen him in Resus, looking all bloodied and battered. 'You gave me a real scare when I saw you in Resus tonight,' she blurted out.

'Sorry. I hadn't realised what a state I was in, although I got off pretty lightly all things considered.'

'You did.' Zoë shivered as she thought about what could have happened. She had no idea what she would do if she lost Ben. She drew herself up short, knowing how dangerous it was to think like that. She'd sworn she would get through the next few months by relying on herself and that's what she must do.

'It wasn't only that which upset you, was it, Zoë?'

Ben's tone was level enough, but her heart jerked painfully. He had always been very astute so had he realised that she'd been upset by the thought that his desire to take care of her stemmed from concern for their baby? Maybe it was silly to let it bother her, but she couldn't help wishing that he would put her first.

'You're right, it wasn't,' she said hurriedly, wanting to dispel the idea as fast as she could. There was no future for her and Ben other than that of parents. 'It was that case we discussed with you, little Bethany Morris.'

'You got the results of the blood tests?' he said, apparently accepting her explanation.

'We did.' Zoë breathed easier, relieved that she'd got away with it. She didn't want Ben to think that she cared how he felt about her—that wouldn't be fair. She should just be glad that he felt so strongly about their child that he was prepared to do everything it took to protect it. 'They showed an excessive amount of white blood cells, roughly thirty times the normal level. There was also a significant number of blast cells present.'

'You're thinking it could be acute lymphoblastic leukaemia?'

'It points that way, doesn't it?'

'Sadly, yes, it does. It tends to occur in kids of Bethany's age, too. It's far more common in the fives and under than in any other age group.' He sighed. 'I expect the parents were gutted when you told them.'

'They were.' She could feel all the emotions welling up inside her again as she recalled the parents' distress, and stood up. 'Anyway, enough about work. I'll take these through to the kitchen and wash them before I go to bed.'

'Put them in the dishwasher,' Ben told her, standing up to open the door. He followed her into the kitchen, leaning against the doorjamb as he watched her stack the crockery in the machine. 'Are you OK, Zoë? A case like that is bound to have hit you hard.'

'I'm fine.' She straightened up and shrugged. 'I can't allow myself to go to pieces over every patient I treat.'

'No-o-o…'

The scepticism in his voice made her bristle. She didn't want his pity—it was the last thing she needed. 'I said I'm fine, Ben.'

'Of course.'

He stepped aside to let her pass and if she hadn't known him so well she'd have thought he believed her. However, one glance at his face was enough to tell her differently. Zoë chose to ignore it rather than get into an argument that neither of them could win. 'I'll get off to bed, then.'

'Before you go we need to decide what we're going to tell everyone.'

'About what?' she asked, pausing.

'Us. The baby. Your treatment.' He sighed. 'I'm sorry if I said more than I should have done tonight, but people will soon find out that you're living here. It won't be long before they find out that you're pregnant either,' he said, his eyes dropping to her stomach.

'I realise that.' Zoë felt a shaft of heat run through her. She knew it was silly to feel self-conscious but she couldn't help it. Ben only had to look at her and she was aware of her body in a way that she normally wouldn't have been.

She chased away the thought. Ben was thinking about their baby, not her. 'I imagine it will be easier if we tell them the truth. I'm sure some people remember that we used to be an item so it won't come as a complete surprise to everyone.'

'If that's what you want, it's fine by me. What about your chemo, though? Are we going to be above board about that too?'

'I don't think we have a choice,' Zoë said bluntly. 'Once I start the treatment, I'll need to take time off, plus the staff on the oncology unit know who I am. I'd rather tell people than have them gossiping behind my back.'

'Good. I'm glad you prefer to be up-front about it.' He shrugged. 'I wasn't looking forward to having to lie, to be honest.'

'I would never expect you to do that, Ben,' she declared fiercely. She saw the surprise on his face and hurried on. 'You're not someone who lies and I'd hate to put you in the position of having to do so for my sake.'

'Thank you for saying that. I've always tried to be open and honest in everything I do.'

There was something in his voice that made her look at him and her heart ached when she saw the regret in his eyes. Ben had never lied to her either: he had been completely honest about his feelings for her too. It had been her own fear that had made her refuse to believe him.

There was nothing Zoë could say to make amends. She simply murmured goodnight and went to her room. She took a shower then slipped on some pyjamas and climbed into bed, but sleep was a long time coming. She kept thinking about the mess she had made of everything.

She placed her hand on her stomach, cradling the precious

new life growing inside her. All she could do was hope that her child would be strong and healthy when it was born. It would be her gift to Ben, something that might make up for the way she had hurt him. Her dearest wish was to see her child grow up, but if it wasn't to be, at least she knew her baby would have a father who adored it.

CHAPTER TEN

BEN sensed a certain buzz in the air when he went in to work the following morning, but he was too tired to wonder what was behind it. He'd barely slept. Knowing that Zoë was lying awake in the next room had made it impossible to sleep. Every time he'd heard her turn over in her bed, he'd had to stop himself getting up and going to her. She needed some space, time to deal with what was happening to her.

There was a bit of a rush shortly after he arrived. A collision between two buses in the high street resulted in a number of people being ferried to the hospital. Thankfully, no one was seriously injured so they were soon dealt with and sent on their way. Abby Blake, the senior nurse on duty that morning, popped her head round the treatment-room door as Ben was finishing off suturing a cut on a patient's forehead.

'Phone call for you, Ben. Shall I ask them to hold or phone back later?'

'I'll just be a couple more seconds so they may as well hold on.' Ben finished off the last stitch and smiled at the young woman. 'That should be fine now. The nurse will cover it with a dressing so try to keep it dry for the next few days. Your GP will remove the stitches so you won't need to come back here.'

'Will it leave a scar?' the girl demanded anxiously, taking a mirror out of her bag and peering into it.

'Nothing significant. It's a very small cut, plus the fact that it's so high up—almost in your hairline—means that nobody will notice it,' he assured her, but she wasn't convinced.

'But when I wear my hair pulled back, it's bound to show.' She shuddered. 'I can't bear the thought that I'm going to be scarred!'

'At the very most all you'll be left with is a tiny white line,' Ben said firmly, trying to curb his impatience. Bearing in mind the number of people who had to face far worse than a minor cut, her reaction seemed way over the top.

The thought reminded him of what Zoë had to face and he swung round before he said something he shouldn't. Turning to Barbara Roberts, the nurse who had assisted him, he asked her to make sure the patient had the requisite form to hand to her GP. Barbara gave him a sympathetic smile as she acknowledged his instructions and he frowned, wondering what he had done to deserve it. Surely he didn't look that frazzled?

The phone call was from the police, who wanted to check his statement about the accident. Ben cleared up a few points and hung up. It appeared the lorry driver had been using his mobile phone at the time of the collision and the police were planning to prosecute him. Ben had checked to see how the driver was doing when he'd got in that morning and although the man was in a serious condition, it looked like he'd survive. Jason was coming out of the cubicles when Ben left the office and he paused.

'Abby said the police were on the phone for you, Ben. Was it about the accident?'

'Yes, they wanted to check a few points in my statement because they're planning to prosecute the lorry driver,' Ben explained.

'I see.' Jason grimaced. 'I suppose you'll end up having to go to court to give evidence, and that's the last thing you need at the moment.'

Ben saw the sympathetic look the nurse gave him and realised that there was definitely something going on. He had a nasty suspicion he knew what it was, too. However, it wasn't until his coffee-break that he had confirmation that he had correctly sussed out the situation. Sam Kearney came into the staffroom and headed straight over to him.

'I was really sorry to hear about Zoë's problems. If there's anything Anna and I can do to help, you only have to ask.'

Ben nodded his thanks, knowing that the other man meant every word. Sam and his wife Anna, who had been a consultant in obs and gynae before the birth of their son, were lovely people. 'Thanks, Sam. I know Zoë will appreciate it when I tell her, too. At the moment she's trying to cope the best way she can but it isn't easy. Being pregnant and having cancer...well, what can I say?'

'Pregnant?' Sam looked at him in horror. 'I knew about the cancer. One of the staff on the oncology unit let it slip that Zoë's a patient there so everyone knows, but I had no idea she was pregnant.'

'Yes. Nightmare scenario, isn't it?' Ben managed to smile but just putting it into words made him feel sick. He took a deep breath. If Zoë could deal with this, so could he. 'Still, everyone is being very positive. The consensus is that the baby will be fine so we just have to trust them, don't we?'

'There's not much else you can do.' Sam lowered his voice as a couple more people came in for their breaks. 'Are you telling folk about the baby?'

'Yes. We won't be able to keep it a secret for very long and Zoë says that she wants to be completely above board about it all.'

'It will make life easier,' Sam agreed then changed the subject to the new car he was considering buying. Ben responded as best he could, although his mind was only half on the merits of the various models. It was a relief when Jason came to fetch him to see a patient.

The rest of the morning flew past. Ben had an inter-departmental meeting scheduled for lunchtime and he had left before Zoë arrived. He didn't catch up with her until the middle of the afternoon and it was too busy to chat then. They'd had an elderly woman brought in with a broken hip and they dealt with that together. By the time the old lady was ready to go to Theatre to have her hip pinned, it was time for Ben to leave, but he didn't want to go without warning Zoë that people knew what was happening.

'Can I have a word, Zoë?' he said as they left Resus. He led her to an alcove that housed the drinks machines. There was nobody about for a change and he stopped there. 'Folk have found out that you're being treated in the oncology unit,' he said, cutting straight to the chase.

'I see. Well, it was bound to happen at some point,' she said with a shrug. Ben couldn't help noticing how pale she looked that day but knew he mustn't fuss and didn't remark on it.

'The only person who knows about the baby so far is Sam Kearney. I told him this morning.'

'That was going to come out too. We already decided that we were going to be up-front about it, Ben.'

'Yes. But I just wanted you to know so that you weren't caught on the hop, so to speak.'

'I appreciate that. Thanks.'

She turned to go but he couldn't let her walk away when he was so concerned about her. Catching hold of her hand, he drew to a halt. 'Are you feeling all right?' He forestalled her reply by holding up his hand. 'I promise I'm not going to fuss over you all the time but you do look washed out today.'

'Thanks a bunch,' she replied tartly, and he grimaced.

'Sorry, but it's true. Did you have a rough night? I know I found it difficult to sleep. My head seemed to be buzzing all night long.'

'I'm sorry, Ben. It's my fault, isn't it? If I hadn't come back here, then you wouldn't be having to go through this.'

He heard the regret in her voice and it was the last thing he wanted to hear. 'None of this is your fault, Zoë. You didn't ask to be ill, did you?'

'No, but getting pregnant as well…' She tailed off, looking so miserable that his heart ached for her.

'Do you wish you'd decided not to have the baby now?' he said softly, knowing that he had to give her the choice even though he couldn't bear to think of the alternative. Zoë's health was the main issue here. Her life was at stake, and that was too important to dismiss.

'No. If I'm honest, it's the only thing that's keeping me going.' She smiled. 'It's like a carrot being dangled in front of me. I keep telling myself that if I can get through the chemo, I'll have a baby at the end of it. That makes it all worthwhile.'

Her bravery took his breath away. Ben couldn't find the words to explain how it made him feel so he resorted to actions instead. Pulling her into his arms, he held her close, hoping she could tell how much he admired her courage. She let him hold her for a moment then gently freed herself.

'I'd better get back before they send out a search party.'

'Fingers crossed you have an easy night,' he replied with what he hoped was the right amount of levity. It was difficult to tell if he'd hit the mark and he didn't hang around to find out. He went up to his office and collected the pile of medical journals he'd been planning on reading for ages and had never got round to. He needed to fill in his evening. He couldn't spend it waiting for Zoë to get home.

He grimaced. Home wasn't how he would describe the apartment, was it? It was merely somewhere to eat and sleep in between going to work. He hadn't had a real home since Zoë had left him, in fact. What was going to happen after the baby was born? he wondered suddenly. Would he carry on living in the apartment; would Zoë continue to live there too? They'd not discussed the future so he had no idea what she planned on doing.

Just for a moment Ben allowed himself the luxury of imagining how different it would have been if they'd still been together as a couple. After the baby was born they would have been a real family. It was something he had dreamed about in the past and it was only too easy to recall all the plans he'd made for them. However, everything was very different now, uncertain, scary. All of a sudden he was glad that he couldn't see into the future. He didn't want to look too far ahead when life was so very fragile. He would just be grateful that Zoë was with him now.

Zoë's chemotherapy began the following Monday. She was dreading it, fearful of how it would make her feel, but more importantly what it could do to her baby. She'd had a scan and had pinned the resulting photo on the notice-board in the kitchen so that she had something to focus on. Every time she made herself a drink she studied the picture of her child, tracing the curve of its head, its tiny limbs, the line of its spine, which looked for all the world like a string of precious pearls. It was too early to determine its sex but that didn't matter. It was proof that it was alive and well, and that was her reason for getting through the next few months, no matter how gruelling they proved to be.

Deborah Gaston met her at the oncology unit shortly before eight o'clock, briskly efficient as she outlined what would happen that day. 'You may not suffer any ill-effects today—some patients don't after their first session. However, the effect of the drugs is cumulative and you must prepare yourself for that. You will have good days and bad. Some days you may wish that you'd never agreed to have the treatment. However, both Mr Walker and I are confident that you will deliver a healthy baby at the end of it.'

'That's the main thing,' Zoë agreed quietly. 'I will never forgive myself if anything happens to this child.'

'Nothing is going to happen to it,' Deborah said firmly.

Deborah introduced her to the nurse who would be monitoring her while she received the first dose of chemotherapy. Zoë said hello, hoping she didn't look as nervous as she felt. She was a doctor and it wasn't right that she should get so worked up.

Sarah, her nurse, smiled at her after Deborah left. 'It's OK to feel apprehensive, Zoë. Everyone feels the same when they first come here.'

'I should be able to deal with it better than most, though, shouldn't I?' Zoë replied with a grimace.

'Because you're a doctor?' Sarah shook her head. 'It doesn't work like that. While you're in here, you are a patient and you're allowed to feel scared. Don't add to the pressure by trying to put on a "professional" front.'

Zoë laughed when the other woman drew imaginary speech marks around the word *professional*. 'All right. I won't.'

Sarah set up the infusion and made sure that Zoë was comfortable then left her to check on another patient. The unit was surprisingly busy even though it was still quite early. Zoë looked around the room, liking what she saw. The walls were painted sunshine yellow and there were colourful prints dotted about. There were pot plants too and their vivid green foliage added to the overall picture of cheerfulness. It certainly wasn't a place laden down by doom and gloom and she felt her spirits lift. Maybe it wouldn't be so bad after all.

There was a stack of magazines beside her chair so she selected one and settled down to read the latest celebrity gossip. When she heard footsteps crossing the room, she didn't immediately look up.

'So this is how you spend your time, is it? Catching up on all the tittle-tattle.'

Zoë gasped when she looked up and found Ben standing in front of her. 'What are you doing here?'

'I thought I'd come and see how you were getting on.' He pulled up a chair, grimacing as he looked at the magazine. 'You don't really enjoy that rubbish, do you?'

'It isn't rubbish,' she said defensively. 'There's some interesting articles in here.'

'Oh, yes?' He regarded her mockingly. 'Who's dating whom and who's having whose baby—that's *really* interesting.'

'You seem to be rather well versed in what's between the covers,' she pointed out and he shifted uncomfortably.

'My youngest sister, Libby, reads all those magazines so they're always lying around the house whenever I go to visit my parents.'

'And you can't help taking a look, purely for interest's sake, of course.'

'Of course,' he replied drolly, his hazel eyes dancing with laughter at being caught out.

Zoë laughed as well. 'You tell a good tale, Ben Nicholls, I'll give you that. You're as keen to know the latest gossip as everyone else is!'

'OK, OK.' He held up his hands in surrender. 'Guilty as charged, your honour. You've uncovered my deepest, darkest secret.'

His eyes met hers and Zoë felt a rush of warmth invade her when she saw the way he was looking at her. It would be so easy to imagine that he still cared about her, and maybe he did too. After all she was the mother of his unborn child and that must count for something.

She glanced down at the magazine so that he wouldn't see how much the idea upset her. She didn't doubt that Ben was concerned because she was ill, but he would feel the same about anyone who found themselves in this position. It was sympathy that made him so attentive to her needs, not love, and that's what hurt. She may have left him two years ago but she had never stopped loving him. She never would.

'So how's it going so far?' Ben's voice cut into her thoughts and Zoë hurriedly collected herself.

'Not too badly. Deborah Gaston said that the effects of the drugs may not kick in immediately so I'll have to wait and see.'

'Are you coming in to work after you finish here?'

'Yes. I want to keep everything as normal as possible.'

Ben sighed. 'I understand that but will you promise me one thing?'

'And that is?' she asked cautiously.

'That if it gets too much for you, you'll take some time off.' He leant forward and she could see the plea in his eyes. 'I don't want you knocking yourself out, Zoë. It won't help you or the baby.'

She knew he was right, but she couldn't afford to let him take over her life. 'All right, I promise, Ben, but only if you'll promise to let me make the decision. I don't want you nagging me all the time.'

'I won't.' He stood up abruptly and returned the chair to where he'd got it from. 'I'll see you later, then.'

He left before she could say anything else, not that there was much more to say. Ben obviously wasn't happy about leaving her to conduct her life the way she saw fit, but that was how it had to be. Maybe he thought she was wrong to shut him out, but she was trying to protect him as well as herself. The next few months were going to be stressful enough without him feeling that he had to worry about her as well as their baby. She had hurt him enough and she didn't intend to hurt him any more if she could avoid it.

Zoë's determination to shut him out of her life as much as she possibly could was very difficult to accept. Over the following weeks, as the effects of her chemotherapy became increasingly apparent, Ben found it hard not to intervene. Some days she looked so worn out that he wanted to order her home to bed, but he knew he would be overstepping the mark if he did that. He comforted himself with the thought that at least she was still living in the apartment, which meant he could keep an eye on her.

March gave way to April and the weather improved almost overnight. Clear skies and sunshine brought a steady flow of visitors to Dalverston. There were a lot of hill walkers and ramblers about and, consequently, the emergency department was busier than ever. Ben lost count of the number of sprained ankles they treated. They were carrying several vacancies and some days they were pushed to the limit. He found himself working longer and longer hours, although that wasn't a bad thing. At least, while he was working, he wasn't worrying about Zoë.

One Thursday evening he was getting ready to leave when a call came through from the Incident Control centre to say there'd been an accident about ten miles outside the town. A helicopter ferrying a group of people home from the races at Haydock Park had crashed in the hills. There was no information yet about the number of casualties, but with Dalverston

General being the nearest hospital to the site of the crash they would take the bulk of the injured. Ben called the team together and explained what had happened.

'So far we don't know how many people have been injured or how severe their injuries are. However, this type of accident can result in anything ranging from broken bones to burns if the helicopter caught fire.' He looked around the group, not allowing his gaze to linger on Zoë. He had to treat her as part of the team. 'Basically, it means that we need to prepare for every eventuality.'

'Has the rapid response unit been deployed?' Jo asked.

'Not yet. Incident Control will get back to me once they've spoken to the police…' He broke off when the phone rang. It was Incident Control again with more information, which he relayed to the group after he hung up.

'The helicopter was carrying six people, including the pilot. The mountain rescue team has now pinpointed the exact location where it crashed and they are about to retrieve the injured. The rapid response unit has been officially deployed and we shall meet them at a prearranged spot as close to the site as possible.' Picking up the daily roster, he skimmed through it. 'I'll be going and, Jason, you will too. Abby, you can come along as well—we'll leave Jo here to sort everything out for when we get back.'

'Thank heavens for that,' Jo retorted. 'I had my hair done this morning and I don't fancy scrambling up the side of a mountain and ending up with the windswept look!'

Everyone chuckled as she patted her hair. Ben grinned. 'And may I say how very nice it looks too.'

He jotted Jason's and Abby's names on the clipboard then checked the roster again. He really needed another doctor to go with them but Sam was tied up in Resus and he didn't want to drag him away. That left Zoë but he was loath to include her in view of everything else.

'I'd like to come along.'

Her voice cut through his musing and Ben looked up, a refusal already forming on his lips until he caught sight of her expression. She was daring him to say that she couldn't go and he knew that if he did so it would result in an argument, which would only upset her. Talk about finding himself stuck between a rock and a hard place!

'Fair enough,' he said evenly, adding her name to the list. He checked that everyone knew what they were doing then led the way to the supply room, trying to batten down his anxiety. So long as he made sure that Zoë didn't do too much, she should be fine.

It didn't take them long to get kitted up in their outdoor gear, which consisted of fluorescent yellow and green waterproof jackets worn with matching trousers. Abby grimaced as she plonked a safety helmet on her head.

'Not exactly what you'd call high fashion, is it?'

'Oh, I don't know.' Jason leered at her. 'It definitely does something for me!'

He dodged out of the way when Abby shook her fist at him. Ben followed them out of the room, wistfully thinking how much he would have loved to joke with Zoë that way. Since the day she'd had her first chemo session and made it clear that she didn't want him poking his nose into her affairs, he'd felt as though he'd been walking on eggshells around her.

'Abby and Jason seem to get on very well. Do I detect a hint of romance in the air?'

He glanced round when Zoë fell into step with him, feeling his emotions see-saw as they always did whenever she was near. Although she looked incredibly fragile at the moment, she was still the most beautiful woman he had ever seen. That hadn't changed, neither would it.

'Possibly, although I should point out that Jason has enjoyed more romantic liaisons with the female members of staff than most people have had hot dinners,' he replied, trying to deflect his thoughts away from such a pointless direction.

Zoë laughed. 'I see. And is Abby one of his conquests?'

'I don't think so.' Ben frowned. 'That's odd. I'd have thought she would have been top of his list.'

'Maybe he doesn't see her as just one of the many.'

'You could be right.' He looked at her in surprise. 'How come you're so clued up when it comes to relationships?'

'I wish I was.'

She gave him a quick smile before she hurried on ahead. Ben followed her over to the rapid response vehicle they'd be using that night, a four-wheel drive equipped with the very latest technology. Jason offered to drive so Ben tossed him the keys and climbed into the passenger seat. Zoë and Abby were sitting in the back and he could hear them chatting as they left the hospital.

What had she meant by that comment? he wondered. Did she wish that she'd been more clued up when it had come to *their* relationship and done something to save it? Even though he knew it was too late to worry about it now, it was a tantalising thought.

CHAPTER ELEVEN

THE mountain rescue team had managed to retrieve two of the casualties by the time they arrived. Zoë jumped out of the vehicle and hurried over to where a makeshift treatment area had been set up. Canvas screens provided welcome shelter from the wind but it was bitterly cold despite the recent improvement in the weather. Ben followed her and he knelt down beside her.

'Let's see what we've got,' he said, turning back the foil blanket that was helping to warm up the first casualty, a girl in her teens.

'Oh, that looks nasty,' Zoë murmured when she saw the section of bone that was poking through the girl's right shin. She smiled at her. 'Hi, my name's Zoë and I'm a doctor. Can you tell me your name and how you came to be in the helicopter?'

'Grace Southern, and I was hitching a lift back home to Carlisle. My brother's a jockey, you see, and I went to watch him race. He drove me down there but he's racing again tomorrow and couldn't take me back. Peter arranged for me to travel back with a friend of his.' She bit her lip. 'It was my first trip in a helicopter and I was so excited about it, too, but I don't think I'll be going in one again.'

'It must have been really scary for you,' Zoë sympathised. 'Try not to think about it right now. I'm going to make you comfortable and then have you transferred to hospital. Obviously, your leg is broken but can you tell me if you hurt anywhere else?'

'All over.' Grace grimaced. Even though she was in a lot of pain, she tried to put on a brave face. 'I feel as though I've been tossed around in a tumble dryer and spat out at the end of the cycle!'

'Ouch!' Zoë winced. 'Sounds horrible. I'll just check you over and make sure there's nothing else before I deal with that leg.'

She quickly examined the girl but apart from some spectacular bruising she couldn't find anything else wrong with her, although it would need X-rays to confirm that. Ben had moved to the second casualty, a man in his forties who had suffered a head injury. He was unconscious and she could tell that Ben was concerned when he looked over at her.

'We need to get him to hospital, asap. Left pupil is fixed and dilated so it looks as though there's intercranial bleeding.'

'When are the ambulances expected to arrive?' Zoë asked as she dealt with her patient's injuries. A shot of morphine for the pain would help to make the girl more comfortable so she administered that first then unwrapped a sterile dressing and placed it carefully over the end of the bone to minimise the risk of infection.

Ben checked his watch. 'It'll be another fifteen minutes at least.' He glanced at the man. 'I'm not sure if he'll last that long. I know it's a risk but I think he'll have a better chance if we ferry him back in the four-by-four.'

Zoë could tell he wasn't completely happy with that idea either. Weighing up the pros and cons of moving the man or waiting for an ambulance wasn't easy but she knew he would make the right decision. She padded the area around where the bone had broken through the flesh then used an inflatable splint to stabilise the girl's leg. Fortunately the drugs had kicked in by then so Grace wasn't in too much pain. Jason and Abby had finished unloading their supplies and they came over to help. Jason treated the girl to a killer smile.

'That's going to be a real talking point amongst your friends.'

Grace blushed as she took stock of the young male nurse's handsome face. 'I'll get them all to sign it if I have a cast on… Will they put a cast on it?' she asked, turning to Zoë.

'It depends what the orthopaedic surgeon decides is the best way to treat it,' Zoë explained, deciding not to go into the ins and outs of whether the leg would need external fixation to hold the bone in place. It could be a daunting prospect and she didn't want to alarm the girl when she appeared to be coping so well.

'Well, if you do end up with a cast then I bag first go at signing it,' Jason said, winking at Grace.

Ben rolled his eyes. 'Some people have no shame, that's all I can say. Right, we need to get this guy out of here pronto and see what's happening further up the hill.'

Jason fetched a specially adapted stretcher that fitted into the rear of the rapid response vehicle once the seats were lowered. Using a padded head restraint to minimise the risk of further injury, they lifted the man onto it and loaded him on board. Abby volunteered to drive him back so Jason handed over the keys. Ben radioed back to base and explained what had happened, emphasising how serious the situation was. With a bit of luck the casualty would be in Theatre within the hour.

Once Abby had departed, one of the rescue team offered to escort them to the crash site. The helicopter had come down at a point halfway up the mountainside and Ben guessed it would be a tough climb to get there. Instinct told him to leave Zoë down below, but he knew they would both be needed. His gaze rested on her for a moment as he struggled with his conscience.

There were people needing their help but was it right to expect Zoë to make the climb in her condition?

He sighed. There wasn't time to debate the issue, but as soon as they got back, he and Zoë were going to have a long talk about what she could be safely expected to do. And if she didn't see sense then he was prepared to pull rank and stop her pushing herself so hard. He'd done enough tiptoeing. It was time he acted.

Zoë could feel Ben looking at her and knew that he was debating whether or not she should be allowed to make the climb. She was quite prepared to argue her case if need be, but in the end he didn't stop her. It should have felt like a victory but she couldn't help the shiver that ran through her as she looked up at the mountain. Was she really up to the task of climbing that slope?

In the past week her treatment had seemed to sap her strength so that it had been an effort to keep going. She'd also been sick on several occasions, although she'd managed to conceal the fact from everyone else, including Ben. What with being pregnant and undergoing chemotherapy, she wasn't exactly in tip-top condition. She could be more of a hindrance than a help, but if she cried off, it would feel as though she was giving up. She took a deep breath. One way or another she was going up that mountain!

It was a tough climb and even Ben had difficulty in places. Zoë was in front of him and he could hear the laboured sound of her breathing as she struggled on. This was madness! he thought savagely. What was she trying to prove? That she could cope with anything? Or, more likely, that she could cope without help and especially not his?

It was another five minutes before they reached the crash

site. Ben sucked in a welcome breath as he took stock of the scene. The helicopter was lying on its side. The tail had sheered off on impact, leaving a gaping hole in the fuselage through which the rescue team had gained entry. There were two bodies lying on the ground, covered by blankets, and a man sitting slumped against a tree. That meant there must be one casualty still inside the helicopter. Turning to the others, Ben rapped out instructions.

'Jason, you come with me and we'll see what's going on inside. Zoë, you attend to that guy. He can be taken down to wait for the ambulances if he's fit enough to be moved.'

He didn't give her time to object as he strode over to the helicopter. Enough was enough and there was no way that he was allowing her to endanger herself any further by crawling inside the wreckage. Two members of the rescue team were trying to free the pilot when Ben worked his way inside the fuselage. The instrument panel had been stoved in, pinning the man to his seat. Ben introduced himself then crouched down in the narrow gap between the seats.

'How long will it take to get him out of there?'

'Hard to say, Doc. We could do with some heavy-duty cutting gear but I don't rate our chances of getting it up here,' one of the rescuers explained, working away with a pair of metal bolt cutters. He managed to cut through a small section of the panel but there was another section underneath that had to be dealt with next.

Ben frowned. 'This could take a while and I'm worried about the effect of all that metal bearing down on him. Can I take a look and see what's going on?'

He traded places with one of the rescuers so that he could peer beneath the overhang of metal. The pilot's left leg was twisted sideways, his foot lying at a right angle to the leg. No doubt the ankle was broken and there was probably ligament damage too, although that wasn't Ben's main concern. Crush syndrome, a condition in which the damaged muscles release excessive amounts of protein pigments into the bloodstream, causing the kidneys to fail, was a very real possibility. Then there was reperfusion injury, inflammation and oxidative damage caused to the tissues when the blood supply was restored. He gently tested the pilot's legs, more concerned than ever when he discovered how swollen they felt as it wasn't a good sign.

He and Jason fixed up a drip to compensate for the drop in blood volume and moved out of the way. By the time the last section of metal was removed, Ben was desperate to get the pilot out.

'We'll be as careful as possible but this could hurt,' he warned him. He'd given the man a shot of morphine but it wasn't an easy procedure to remove him from the helicopter. As soon as they were outside, Ben explained what he wanted doing.

'Zoë, I want you to deal with that ankle. Jason, I need a second line in as soon as we've got him on the stretcher. Let's get a move on. We want him in hospital like yesterday.'

Everyone did their very best and in a remarkably short time they were on their way. There were a lot of willing hands to help but it was tough going. Ben carried one end of the stretcher while Jason held both drips. Zoë was following behind but he didn't dare take his eyes off the path to check that she was all right. He would have to hope that she was being careful but this was the last time she was coming out on a shout.

They made it down to the road in one piece and Ben was relieved to see an ambulance waiting. Abby had returned and she offered to drive Jason and Zoë back while he accompanied the pilot. Ben just caught a glimpse of Zoë's white face as he climbed into the ambulance but it was enough to strengthen his determination. She could protest all she liked, but she couldn't carry on like this: he wouldn't let her!

By the time they reached the hospital, Zoë felt dreadful. It took her all her time to clamber out of the vehicle and follow the others inside. Abby held the door open, grinning as Jason staggered inside, loaded down with their equipment.

'Good to see him doing something useful for a change, isn't it, Zoë?'

'It is.' Zoë summoned a smile but it demanded an awful lot of effort and Abby looked at her in concern.

'You look terribly pale. Why don't you go and have a cup of tea? It might perk you up.'

'That would be great, so long as you don't think I'm deserting you,' Zoë replied gratefully.

'No way!' Abby lowered her voice. 'I think you're really brave, Zoë. If it was me having to undergo chemo, I'd have signed myself off work. You're a real trouper, in my opinion.'

Zoë was deeply touched and felt her eyes fill with tears. 'Thanks,' she said, turning away before the other woman noticed them. She dumped her protective clothing in the bin to be cleaned and headed for the staffroom. A cup of tea would help to revive her and then she would go back to finish her shift…

A wave of nausea washed over her and she dashed into the lavatories. By the time she'd finished throwing up, she felt totally drained. She rinsed her face under the cold tap then stared into the mirror over the basin. What a sight she looked! Her face was paper-white, her hair sticking in clumps to her forehead, and the black circles around her eyes made her look like a panda. All of a sudden it was all too much and tears began to flow down her cheeks. She didn't know how she was going to get through this!

She didn't hear the door open, didn't hear Ben's footsteps as he crossed the room. The first she knew was when he pulled her into his arms. Zoë clung to him, needing his strength to support her both physically and mentally.

'It's all right, sweetheart. Don't cry. It's going to be OK, I promise you.'

He whispered the words in her ear and Zoë longed to believe them, but there was no guarantee he was right. Her treatment might work but it might not and then what would happen? It wasn't fair to expect him to look after her as well as their baby. Stepping back, she deliberately freed herself and him from the emotional bonds.

'Sorry. I'm a bit overwrought at the moment.'

'Overwrought isn't how I'd describe it, Zoë.' His expression was grim. 'You're wearing yourself out because you're too stubborn to accept that you need to slow down and let people help you.'

'I know what I'm doing,' she said sharply, attempting to step around him. The last thing she felt like doing was arguing when they were bound to disagree. She didn't have the strength.

'Do you?' Ben stepped in front of her. 'This is what you would recommend if you had a patient who was pregnant and undergoing chemotherapy, is it? You'd advise her to keep pushing herself to exhaustion point to prove she can manage?'

The irony in his voice stung and she glared at him. 'No. I would advise the patient to do what *she* thought was best for *her*, just as I'm doing. This is my way of dealing with the situation, Ben. It has nothing to do with anyone else.'

'And especially not me.' He folded his arms, looking so stern that she quailed inwardly. 'That's the real explanation, isn't it, Zoë? You're so determined to stop me helping you that you'd rather endanger your own health, not to mention the health of our child.'

'How dare you accuse me of that? Everything I've done has been for the sake of this baby.' Her hand went protectively to her stomach but Ben didn't relent.

'I dare because it's true. I thought you were many things, Zoë, but I never thought you were selfish.'

'Selfish,' she echoed numbly.

'Yes. You know that I want to help you, but you won't let me. You prefer to let me worry rather than accept my help.'

'I'm trying to make this easier for you,' she whispered, stricken by the accusation.

'How? By cutting me out? By making it clear that you don't give a damn what I think?' He laughed bitterly. 'I'm sorry, Zoë, but it isn't working. It was the same when we were together before. You never understood that I wanted to share the bad times as well as the good with you.' His eyes grazed over her and she saw the pain they held. 'Obviously, you've never loved anyone enough to understand that, and certainly not me.'

Zoë didn't know what to say. She'd thought she was protecting him when all she'd done had been to cause him more pain. She stood in silence after he left, wondering if he was right. Should she accept his help? Was it kinder to involve him rather than cut him out? Was it what she should have done two years ago, told him the truth and explained her fears?

All of a sudden she realised he was right. It wasn't only the good times that made a relationship work but dealing with the tough times too. That's what she and Ben should have done in the past, but was it what they should do now? Should they deal with this together?

If she knew with absolute certainty that she could beat this terrible illness, she would be tempted—very tempted—but she had no idea what was going to happen. She couldn't see further than the next few months and that wasn't far enough, certainly not enough to offer Ben in return for his help. She couldn't bear the thought that she might become an object of pity to him, a burden. She really couldn't do that to him. So long as she knew that he would be there for their child, it was enough.

CHAPTER TWELVE

BEN had no idea if he had managed to get through to Zoë, although he doubted it. She could be so stubborn when she chose, he thought savagely as he made his way to Resus. All he wanted to do was to help her but he couldn't force her to accept that—she had to realise it herself. And the chances of her doing that at the moment were nil.

Sam was attending to the pilot, and looked up when Ben appeared. 'Urine sample shows a very high concentration of urea and potassium.'

'Obviously his kidney function has been impaired. That's what I was worried about.'

Ben tried to clear his mind as he stopped beside the bed. The pilot's BP, heart rate and oxygen saturation levels were being monitored and he automatically checked the readings. The man's BP was up, his sats were low but, all things considered, he wasn't doing too badly. He'd been fitted with a catheter and Ben checked the output of urine, frowning when he saw how little had collected in the bottle.

'He's going to need dialysis,' he said, glancing at Sam. Out of the corner of his eye he saw the door open and his mouth compressed when he saw Zoë come into the room. What was she doing here? Didn't she have the sense to know when to give up? Or was she so intent on proving that she didn't need his help that she was prepared to push herself to any lengths?

He swung round before Sam could reply and strode across the room. 'You are not needed here, Dr Frost,' he said, his voice sounding so harsh that he scarcely recognised it. He was aware that everything had gone quiet, but he didn't give a damn if people were listening. Zoë's health was his number-one concern, whether she liked it or not. 'You're to go home immediately and unless you look demonstrably better in the morning, I don't want to see you back here. Is that clear?'

'You can't do that.' An angry flush stained her cheeks as she glared at him. 'If I say that I'm fit to work, that's the end of the matter.'

'That's where you're mistaken.' Ben stared back, unwilling to give an inch. 'I am in charge of this department and in my opinion you aren't fit to finish your shift. Either you accept that and go home, or I will take the appropriate steps to terminate your contract.'

She looked at him as though she couldn't believe what she was hearing but he didn't back down. He didn't want to upset her, but sometimes it was necessary to be cruel to be kind. The silence seemed to last for ever as she debated what to do and then she spun round and stalked out of the door.

Ben clamped down on the urge he felt to follow her as he went back to his patient. He wouldn't apologise for what he'd done. Someone had to make Zoë see sense and that someone had to be him. He and Sam had a brief discussion and agreed that the pilot needed to go to the renal unit as soon as his ankle had been seen by the orthopaedic registrar. In the meantime, he would need careful monitoring. It was rather like a juggling act, weighing one procedure against another and hoping that all the balls would stay in the air.

A bit like his life, Ben thought grimly as he signed the patient's notes. He seemed to be forever juggling Zoë's needs against what she would allow him to do for her. He was terrified that at some point all the balls would drop and that would be it. But somehow, some way, he had to keep control for Zoë's sake. She needed him even if she refused to admit it. The fact that he needed to be allowed to help her was something he didn't intend to dwell on, however. He only had to remember their earlier conversation to know how pointless it was. Zoë had never loved him as much as he'd loved her and there was no way that he was prepared to place himself in the position of being hurt again.

Zoë had never felt so angry in her life. That Ben had dared to speak to her like that in front of their colleagues was beyond the pale. Instead of growing calmer on the journey back to the apartment, her temper soared. She'd be damned if she'd allow him to treat her like an *imbecile*!

She went straight to her room and dragged her suitcase out of the wardrobe. Opening the drawers, she bundled her clothes into it then went into the bathroom, scooped up her toiletries, and tossed them in as well. The case seemed to weigh a ton as she hauled it into the sitting room and went to phone for a taxi, but she wasn't going to wait until Ben came home so he could treat her like a half-wit again. She was leaving immediately and she wasn't coming back!

Once the taxi was booked, Zoë felt a little calmer. It was so unlike Ben to behave that way, she thought. He rarely lost his temper and he had never lost it before with her. She sighed. He must have been pushed to the limit to have treated her that way and she couldn't help feeling guilty. Maybe she should have admitted how tired she felt instead of trying to carry on?

By the time the taxi arrived, her anger had fizzled out, leaving her feeling deflated. It didn't help either that she had nowhere to stay, although, hopefully, she would be able to get a room at the hotel tonight. She briefly debated what she would do if that wasn't possible but still hadn't decided when the taxi driver buzzed again to remind her he was waiting. She grimaced as she wheeled her case to the lift. She would have to think of something.

Zoë had just reached the foyer when a car drew up outside and her heart sank when she saw Ben leap out. 'And where do you think you're going?' he demanded, coming to a halt in front of her.

'The hotel.' Zoë propped the heavy glass door open with her elbow while she attempted to drag her suitcase through the gap but, typically, it got stuck halfway.

Ben shook his head as he freed it for her. 'This is silly, Zoë. It's late and you're tired.'

'And I have no intention of staying here and being spoken to the way you spoke to me before.' She whipped up her anger again because it hurt to see the bleakness in his eyes and know she was responsible for it.

'I'm sorry. I know it doesn't make it right but I was worried about you. That's why I reacted the way I did.'

There was no doubting his sincerity but Zoë was afraid that if she wavered now, she would waver again in the future. She didn't want there to be a repeat of tonight, couldn't bear to think that she and Ben would end up arguing again. It was best if she left, cut some of the ties if not them all. After all, it was the baby who needed Ben's help, not her.

'I apologise as well for being so stubborn. I did feel rotten and I should have had the sense to go home.'

'So now that we've sorted that out, won't you come back inside?'

He touched her hand, just briefly with the tips of his fingers as though he was afraid that if he took too big a liberty he would scare her. Maybe he would too, Zoë thought miserably, scare her into doing what she wanted most of all. How she longed to love him and know that he loved her in return. It was time she put the past behind her and enjoyed whatever time she had left, be it long or short. She wanted to let herself love Ben so much that it hurt.

Tears filled her eyes and she blinked them away. Even if there'd been the slimmest chance that Ben returned her feelings, she couldn't have told him how she felt. She couldn't give him her love, ask him to love her, when one day that love might be snatched away.

'I think it's best if I leave, Ben.' She shook her head when he went to interrupt. 'It's not just what happened tonight. It's time I found somewhere else to live rather than impose on you.'

'You aren't imposing on me.' The taxi driver beeped his horn and he glanced impatiently over his shoulder. 'Let me pay off the cab while we discuss this properly. It's a big decision, Zoë, and it's not one you should make in a hurry.'

'No, the decision is already made. I've made it,' she said firmly because he needed to understand that she was determined to see this through. Maybe it had been anger that had driven her to leave, but now she could see it was the best thing to do. 'I appreciate everything you've done for me since I came back to Dalverston but I need my own space. So do you. Living and working together in these circumstances is too stressful.'

'So where will you go?'

He seemed to have accepted her decision and she was grateful for that. 'I'll find a flat as soon as I can. In the meantime, I'll stay at the hotel tonight and book into a B&B in the morning.'

He pulled a face. 'You need somewhere decent to live, Zoë.'

'I know, and I'll be very choosy, I promise you.' She took hold of her case, knowing that if she lingered she wouldn't be able to leave.

'I'll take that.'

Ben carried her case over to the taxi and stowed it in the boot. Zoë rolled down the window, smiling as hard as she could when she saw the worry in his eyes. 'I'll be fine, Ben. Don't worry about me. There's no need.'

'I'll always worry about you, Zoë.' He leant forward and kissed her on the lips. His mouth was so gentle that her heart overflowed with love. It was all she could do not to tell him how she felt when he drew back. 'Take care. You know where I am if you need me.'

He handed the driver a twenty-pound note and told him to take her to the hotel then stepped aside as the taxi set off. Zoë twisted round in her seat to wave but he had already gone inside. She sank back in the seat, wondering if she was mad to leave. She could have stayed with Ben until their baby was born and then… What? Would she have left him then, or would she have found another reason to stay? And another and another? Could she honestly see herself taking their child away from Ben once he got to know it?

All of a sudden it hit her how flawed her original plan had been. She'd seen Ben as a back-up, the person who would take over in the event of her death. Her main concern had been their child's needs, but she hadn't made any allowance for what Ben might need. He wasn't a substitute but a very important part of their son's or their daughter's future, and she could never cut him out.

Zoë took a deep breath, overwhelmed by a sudden feeling of relief. It meant that Ben would always be part of her future too.

* * *

Ben could scarcely believe how badly everything had turned out. As he let himself into the apartment, he could feel the shock ripping him apart. If anything happened to Zoë because of this, he would never forgive himself.

He went to the cupboard where he kept some bottles of spirits and poured himself a stiff whisky. However, one sip was enough to make his stomach roll with nausea. He put down the glass and paced the floor, wondering what to do. There had to be a way to persuade Zoë to come back, but for the life of him he couldn't think how to set about it. He was afraid that anything he said would make the situation worse, although maybe it wouldn't be pushing matters if he checked that she had arrived safely at the hotel.

A few seconds later he was speaking to the receptionist, who assured him that Dr Frost had checked in a short time earlier. Ben thanked her and hung up, deeming it wiser not to ask to be put through to Zoë's room. He had to give her some space, let everything calm down in the hope that she would see sense.

He groaned. What he thought of as sense didn't automatically correspond with Zoë's views, did it? She was an intelligent woman with a mind of her own, and he'd made no allowance for that. No wonder she had decided to leave. She had warned him that she didn't want him interfering and he'd ignored her. He wouldn't blame her if she decided to have as little as possible to do with him from now on. He would still see her at work—for as long as she was well enough to work—but there may be minimal contact beyond that. All he could hope was that she would still allow him to help with the baby when the time came.

Ben let out a gusty sigh. Life had seemed pretty grim when he'd woken up that morning, but it was nothing to how it felt right now!

* * *

Zoë managed to find herself a room in a B&E

morning. It was clean and close to the hospital,

that mattered. The thought of having to look f

daunting one, but she decided to worry about it

At least she had somewhere to stay that wouldn'

It was with some trepidation that she went

lunchtime. Although she still felt tired and slig

she felt better than she had done the previous

concern now was how everyone would react

happened then. Abby was in the staffroom whe

and she greeted her with a sympathetic smile.

'Hi! How are you feeling? You look a lot better th

yesterday, I must say.'

'I feel better too,' Zoë stated firmly, hanging up he

She followed Abby out of the room, pausing when the

woman stopped.

'Everyone understands how worried Ben is, so don't fee

awkward about what happened yesterday, Zoë. Nobody will

make a big deal of it, I promise you.'

'That's good to hear,' Zoë said thankfully. Abby was right

because everyone treated her as they always did. By the time Ben

arrived back from his lunch, she felt more relaxed and it showed.

'You look much better today,' he said as he came over to her.

'I feel better,' she said simply. 'I overdid it yesterday but I won't

make that mistake again. I intend to pace myself from now on.'

'Good.'

He left it there, not even asking her if she'd managed to book

into the hotel the previous night and, perversely, Zoë felt a

little put out by his lack of interest. She dismissed the thought

by telling herself that she was being ridiculous. She was the one

who had decided to strike out on her own and it had been the

right thing to do.

ernoon flew past. Fractured limbs and sprains seemed
order of the day and Zoë lost track of the number of
he sent for X-rays. She was due to have another round
otherapy that afternoon and had timed her appointment
ncide with her teabreak. She made her way to the
gy unit and booked in. She had just sat down when she
Mr and Mrs Morris, Bethany's parents, coming along the
dor. They recognised her immediately and stopped.

'It's Dr Frost, isn't it?' Alison exclaimed.

'That's right.' Zoë stood up. 'How are you both? And how's
ethany?' She sighed. 'I followed up her case so I know that she's
een diagnosed with acute lymphoblastic leukaemia. I'm so sorry.'

'She's so-so at the moment,' Steve replied sadly. 'The chemotherapy has knocked her for six and they've kept her in, poor
little mite. We spend most of our time here, don't we, Alison?'

'We do.' Alison's eyes filled with tears. 'It's so hard to see
her like this, Dr Frost. Some days she looks so ill.'

'It must be awful for you,' Zoë said quietly, understanding
only too well how devastated they must feel.

'It is. But it's far worse for our Beth.' Alison pulled herself
together and managed a watery smile. 'Are you working here
now? Beth will be thrilled to bits if you are. She never stops
talking about the pretty doctor who read her a story!'

'Really? I'm flattered.' Zoë smiled at the woman. 'Actually,
I'm a patient here. I was diagnosed with breast cancer a couple
of months ago.'

'Oh, dear, I am sorry!' Alison looked genuinely upset and
Zoë hurried to reassure her.

'I'm having treatment and everyone is very positive as to the
outcome.' She could tell that she hadn't managed to convince
the other woman and carried on. 'Would you mind if I popped

in to see Beth? It will be a while before I get called in for my appointment and I'd love to see her again.'

'Of course! She's in the children's unit—it's this way.'

Alison led the way along the corridor to the children's oncology unit. It was bright and noisy and not at all like a place where very sick children were treated. Bethany was at the far end of the ward and her face lit up when she saw Zoë with her parents.

'Hello, poppet, how are you?' Zoë asked, smiling at the little girl.

'I haven't been sick at all today,' Bethany told her gravely. She was extremely pale, her small face showing the effects of her illness and the rigorous treatment she was undergoing, and Zoë's heart went out to her. She knew how awful she felt at times, so how much worse must it be for a child of Bethany's age?

'That's wonderful! What a brave little girl you are.' She gave Bethany a hug, her emotions welling to the surface when she felt the child's thin little arms wrap themselves around her neck.

'Dr Frost is having treatment here as well, Beth,' Steve explained to his daughter. 'She's been poorly too but she's getting better, like you are.'

'Will your hair fall out too?' Bethany asked Zoë curiously. 'The nurse said that my hair may fall out like some of the other children's. It's 'cos of the medicine,' she explained importantly.

'It may do,' Zoë agreed gravely. 'I'll have to wait and see.'

'I hope mine doesn't fall out 'cos my friends will tease me,' Bethany muttered, staring down at the brightly patterned quilt on her bed.

'They may tease you a little at first but I'm sure they won't say anything really horrible because they love you,' Zoë assured her.

It seemed to work because Bethany's face immediately brightened. They chatted for a few more minutes before Zoë excused herself so she wouldn't be late for her appointment, but not before she'd promised to visit Beth again. As she left the children's ward she was more determined than ever that she was going to beat this terrible illness. Seeing how well Bethany was coping had been truly inspiring.

She returned to ED after her treatment and was soon in the thick of things. She was just examining an elderly man's wrist—another suspected fracture—when Abby popped her head round the cubicle curtain.

'RTA on its way, Zoë. ETA five minutes. Ben's tied up in Resus and Sam's doing a split shift so it's your shout. OK?'

'Fine. I'll just finish up in here.'

Zoë sent her patient off to X-Ray and headed to the ambulance bay. She'd just got there when Ben arrived.

'How did it go this afternoon?' he asked, leaning against the wall while they waited for the ambulance to appear.

'Fine. I saw Bethany Morris there—remember her, the child who was brought in with suspected smoke inhalation?'

'Which turned out to be acute lymphoblastic leukaemia.' He shrugged when she looked at him in surprise. 'I checked up to see what had happened about the case.'

'Oh, right. So did I, funnily enough.' Zoë felt warmth ripple through her. Had Ben pursued the case because he'd known it had been important to her? She guessed it was so and hurried on, not wanting him to suspect how touched she felt. 'They're keeping her in because she hasn't been too well so I popped in to see her while I was waiting for my appointment. She's such a brave little thing. I was amazed by how well she's coping.'

'Kids seem to cope really well,' he agreed. 'They have this natural ability to bounce back.'

'I envy them,' she said ruefully.

'You're coping wonderfully well, Zoë. You're an inspiration to everyone.'

There was no time for her to reply because the ambulance arrived just then. However, as Zoë hurried outside to meet it, she couldn't help feeling proud that Ben thought she was managing so well. Maybe she had pushed herself too hard yesterday but she'd learned her lesson and wouldn't do it again, especially when it would only worry him.

She sighed. Was Ben worried about her, though, or the effect it could have on their baby if she did too much? Maybe it was silly to wish that he cared after the way she had hurt him but she couldn't help it. She'd lost something truly special when she'd lost his love and it was something she regretted bitterly.

CHAPTER THIRTEEN

THERE were two people involved in the RTA, a boy of ten and a middle-aged man who had been driving the car that had knocked him down. The boy was their main concern as he had lost consciousness before the ambulance had arrived so Ben and Zoë checked him over together. Zoë opted to stay with him once they had finished their initial examination while Ben went to check on the driver. Adam Sanders had taken the patient's history from the paramedics and he relayed the information to Ben.

'Patient's name is Lawrence Jeffries, aged forty-eight. Suspected MI. No previous history of cardiac trouble, but he's a smoker and admits that he gets very little exercise because of his job. He's a sales rep and spends a lot of time in his car,' Adam added.

'I see. When did he start complaining of chest pain?' Ben queried, adding up everything he'd heard. Smoking greatly increased the chances of a heart attack and when added to the patient's lifestyle—a sedentary, high-pressured job, little or no exercise, plus a diet that probably relied heavily on fast food—you had a recipe for disaster.

'In the ambulance on the way here,' Adam told him.

'Right. He'll need an ECG as well as bloods. And he's going to need the usual cocktail.' Ben rattled off a list of the drugs the

patient needed while Adam wrote them down on the file—
thrombolytics to dissolve any blood clots, analgesics to lessen
the pain and antiarrhythmic drugs to control heart rhythm dis-
turbance which often resulted from a myocardial infarction, or
heart attack as it was more commonly known.

'That's covered all the bases.' He turned to the patient as the
younger doctor hurried away to get everything set up. 'I'm
Ben Nicholls, the consultant in charge of ED. Sorry to talk over
your head but I need to make sure everything necessary has
been done to help you, Mr Jeffries.'

'Fine, fine.' Lawrence Jeffries flapped his hand to indicate
he wasn't bothered and Ben continued.

'How is the pain now? Worse than it was or about the same?'

'About the same.' The man levered himself up so he could
look over to where Zoë was working on the child. 'I didn't see
him, Doctor. One minute the road was clear and the next, he
was in front of me.'

'Don't worry about that now,' Ben said firmly as the man's
BP rose, causing the monitor to beep out a warning. Lawrence
sank back down, clutching his chest and heaving for breath. Ben
took the oxygen mask off its hook and slipped it over his nose
and mouth. 'You must try to stay calm, Mr Jeffries. Breathe
slowly—that's it, nice and steady.'

It was a while before the patient's BP settled down. In the
meantime, the results of the blood test came back. Ben moved
away from the bed while he read them, signalling for Adam
to join him.

'Definitely an MI.' He pointed to the figures. 'There's the
confirmation.'

Adam nodded as he studied the sheet which showed a significant increase in the level of heart enzymes in Lawrence's
blood. This had occurred when the damaged heart muscle

cells had released enzymes into his bloodstream. 'What do we do now?'

'Get on to the cardio team,' Ben said firmly. 'The sooner he gets specialist treatment, the better the outcome for him. They may decide that he needs an angiograph. From the information he's given us, I'd say he's a prime candidate for atherosclerosis. If any of the blood vessels are blocked, the cardiac team may consider a bypass.'

'It could turn out that this actually saves his life,' Adam said in surprise.

'It could indeed.' Ben glanced over his shoulder when he heard a commotion at the other side of the room and frowned when he saw that Zoë was leaning against the wall looking decidedly wobbly. 'Get on to the cardio team and ask them to send someone down here as soon as possible,' he instructed then made his way over to her. 'What's wrong?'

'I just felt a bit faint for a moment, but I feel better now.'

She straightened up but it was obvious from her pallor that she wasn't well. Ben hoped he wouldn't have another fight on his hands, but he couldn't let her attend to a patient if she wasn't up to it. He was about to tell her that as tactfully as he could when she grimaced.

'Can you take over for me?' She shot an anxious look at the boy. 'I don't want to compromise my patient's safety in any way.'

'Of course.' Ben could barely conceal his relief, but he knew that Zoë would hate it if he made a song and dance about her decision. 'Go and have a cup of tea. It will do you good.'

'Thanks. I shall.'

She gave him a quick smile and knew that he had judged her response correctly. It was a real boost, too, after what had happened the previous day. Maybe they were both singing from the same hymn sheet at last?

The thought buoyed him up as he explained to the boy that he was taking over from Dr Frost. Although young Rick Archer had been unconscious when the crew had arrived at the scene, he had come round a few minutes later. There were no obvious signs of serious head trauma—both eyes reacted equally to the light, Rick had been able to tell them his name, age and address, and what he had been doing before the accident. However, he had complained of a headache on the way to the hospital. Zoë had added a note to his file to say she suspected that Rick had concussion and Ben agreed with her, although he couldn't overlook the possibility that there might be a more serious injury.

'I'm going to look into your eyes again, Rick. I know Dr Frost has done this already, but it's essential that we make sure you haven't injured your head too badly.'

'It really hurts where I hit it on the ground,' Rick told him. 'I've got a massive lump there, too. You can feel it.'

The boy turned his head so that Ben could feel the lump above his left ear. Ben gently examined the swelling and nodded.

'That's quite a lump you've got there, young man. How come you didn't see the car?'

Rick bit his lip, obviously loath to answer the question. 'I was texting my friend Charlie,' he muttered finally.

'That wasn't too clever of you, was it?' Ben took the torch out of its holder. 'Next time wait until *after* you've crossed the road before you use your phone. It's a lot safer that way.'

Rick didn't say anything. Ben suspected it was advice he'd been given many times before by his parents. He checked Rick's reaction to light and was pleased to see that both pupils responded normally again. He put the torch back in its holder then asked Rick what day it was and the name of his favourite football team. Rick had no difficulty answering either question which was another encouraging sign, although Ben preferred not to take any chances. He smiled at the boy after he'd finished.

'Right, you've passed all the tests and earned yourself a gold star, but I want to make certain that everything is working properly so I'm going to send you for a CT scan—that's a whizzy sort of X-ray that will give me a three-dimensional image of the inside of your head. It means I'll be able to check that you haven't damaged your skull. OK?'

'Cool! Wait till Charlie hears about this. He'll be well impressed!'

'I'm sure he will. But promise me that you won't text him while you're crossing the road.'

He ruffled the boy's hair then asked the nurse to arrange for a porter to take Rick for his scan. The coronary care registrar had arrived and was talking to Adam so Ben decided he wasn't needed. It meant he could check on Zoë. She was in the staffroom, drinking a cup of weak tea. Ben grimaced as he sat down beside her.

'That looks disgusting.'

'It tastes it too, but it's the only way I can drink tea at the moment. And I can't touch coffee—the smell of it makes me feel nauseous.'

'The joys of pregnancy,' he said lightly, earning himself a wan smile.

'Either that or the result of my chemo. Take your pick.'

'It must be horrible for you,' Ben said quietly. 'If there's anything I can do to help, you know that you only have to tell me, don't you?'

'Yes, I know that. Thank you. It may not seem as though I appreciate how kind you've been but I do, Ben, really.'

'You don't have to thank me, Zoë. I want to help any way I can.'

He saw her mentally withdraw when she heard the emotion

that had crept into his voice and silently cursed himself. Zoë wasn't interested in how he felt and he had to remember that. He stood up abruptly, unable to feign indifference when he most definitely didn't feel indifferent to her plight. 'I'd better get back. I've sent Rick for a CT although I'm pretty sure he's suffering from mild concussion.'

'That's what I thought,' she agreed then returned to her tea.

Ben left her to finish it because there wasn't anything else he could do. It was sheer torture to imagine how awful she must be feeling, but Zoë wouldn't appreciate it if he fussed over her. All she wanted from him was the security of knowing that he would look after their baby.

It should have been enough but he was very much aware that he would have liked to do more than that. He wanted to take care of her too and the thought worried him in view of the fact that he had sworn he would never get involved emotionally again. However, it was hard to remain detached when he could see her suffering, very hard not to feel anything. In his heart he was aware that he felt a lot of things but he was too afraid to put them into words. He didn't think he could bear to have his heart broken again by Zoë. But there again he didn't think he could bear it if he lost her either. As he was realising to his cost, it wasn't easy to keep his emotions in check where Zoë was concerned.

Zoë was bone-tired by the time she left work that night. The latest dose of chemotherapy seemed to have knocked the stuffing out of her. Fortunately, the B&B was within walking distance and she went straight to her room. Although there were no cooking facilities in the rooms, she did have a kettle so she made herself another cup of tea. She knew she should eat for the baby's sake, but she wasn't hungry. She would have to make more of an effort tomorrow.

She was on an early shift the following day so she got up and went to take a shower. It was while she was washing her hair that she noticed there seemed to be an awful lot of hair in the shower tray. There was a great big clump of it in the plughole and another by her feet.

Turning off the water, she hurried to the mirror and gasped. Several large sections of her hair had fallen out, leaving bare patches of skull showing through. And when she ran her fingers through her hair, more came out. Although she'd been warned it could happen, it was still a shock and tears began to stream down her cheeks. On top of everything else, she felt like a freak!

Ben was pouring himself a cup of tea when the doorbell rang and he frowned. It was too early for visitors and the postman didn't normally arrive until the middle of the morning. Getting up, he went to the intercom.

'Yes?'

'It's me, Zoë. Can I come up?'

'Of course.'

Ben pressed the button that unlocked the main doors then hurried to the front door and opened that too. He had no idea what Zoë wanted at this hour of the day but he couldn't help feeling anxious. She appeared a moment later and his anxiety level rose when he realised she'd been crying.

'Come in,' he said, ushering her inside. 'Has something happened, Zoë?'

'I know I'm being silly, but this morning when I was in the shower, I discovered that my hair is falling out.' She took off the scarf she was wearing. 'They did warn me it could happen but it was such a shock…'

She tailed off, trying very hard not to cry, and Ben's heart went out to her. He put his arms around her and hugged her, wishing he could have spared her this heartache. It wasn't fair that she had to suffer this on top of everything else.

She let him hold her for a moment then gently freed herself. 'I decided it would be simpler if I shaved off all my hair rather than lose it in dribs and drabs. I don't think I can manage to do it myself, though, so I was hoping you'd help me.'

'Of course.' Ben refused to think about how painful it was going to be to comply with her request. He had always loved her hair, gloried in its silky texture, its softness, its colour, but if this was what Zoë wanted, he couldn't refuse. 'Do you want me to do it now?'

'Please.' She gave him a tight little smile. 'There's no point putting it off now that I've made up my mind.'

'I'll get my electric razor then. We'll do it in the kitchen. The light's better in there.'

Ben's heart was heavy as he went to collect what he needed. Zoë had placed a chair in front of the window and had covered the floor with newspaper when he went back. She looked up and smiled, and his heart overflowed when he saw the resolve in her eyes. She was so brave that she put him to shame.

Actually shaving off her hair was as bad as he'd feared it would be. As each glossy red-gold strand dropped onto the floor, it felt as though another knife was being driven through him. There was silence when he finished, then Zoë abruptly got up and left the room, and he heard her go into the bathroom and close the door. Ben picked up the newspaper and put it in the bin so that everywhere would be tidy when she came back, which she did a few minutes later. She had wound the scarf around her head to form an elegant turban and he nodded in approval.

'That looks great. More like a fashion statement than anything else.'

'It serves its purpose,' she replied evenly, but he heard the catch in her voice and knew how emotional she must be feeling.

'It certainly does.' Ben turned away before he said something he shouldn't. Zoë didn't want his reassurance that she still looked beautiful, even though it was true. Not even the loss of her hair could alter the fact that he found her desirable.

'How about a cup of tea?' he asked, shaken by the thought.

'Thanks, but I'll give it a miss.' She glanced at her watch. 'I'd better go if I don't want to be late. Thanks for this, Ben. I couldn't have managed it on my own.'

'It wasn't a problem.' Ben picked up his jacket. 'I'll run you in to work. I have a meeting at eight so I was planning on getting there early this morning,' he added to forestall any objections.

They left the apartment and got into the hire car he'd been using since his own had been written off in the crash. However, they'd gone only a couple of hundred yards when they encountered a traffic jam. 'It must be those wretched roadworks again.' Ben groaned. 'It's been murder trying to get through the town centre recently.'

'Everyone's been having trouble,' Zoë murmured and he looked sharply at her when he realised that she was crying.

'Sweetheart!'

'Please, don't be nice to me, Ben. I don't think I can bear it.'

'And I can't bear to know that you're upset and not do anything about it,' he ground out. The traffic started moving again and they carried on for a mile or so without speaking before Zoë sighed.

'I don't want you getting hurt, Ben, or at least not any more than you've been hurt already.'

Ben shook his head. 'My feelings don't matter, Zoë.'

'But they do! If I hadn't come back here, you wouldn't have had to go through all this.'

'No. But I wouldn't have known about the baby, would I?' His heart suddenly lurched. 'Is that what you would have preferred if the circumstances had been different? Would you have opted to exclude me from our child's life if you hadn't needed my help?'

'Of course not! I would never have done that to you, Ben. I would never have done that to our child either. He or she needs you. I'm one hundred per cent sure about that.'

'Thank you.' Ben was so moved that it took him a moment to collect himself. That Zoë saw him as an integral part of their child's future was far more than he'd expected. He'd assumed that she had turned to him out of necessity rather than choice, but maybe that wasn't true.

His mind ran away with the idea, spinning enticing pictures of the future they could have together as a family before he mentally applied the brakes. Zoë might want him involved in their child's life but she'd made it clear that she didn't want him involved in hers.

'D'you know what?' he said, deliberately changing the subject.

'What?'

'I think we both need a spot of R&R.' He kept his eyes on the road so that his mind wouldn't start spinning those fantasies again. He had to settle for what he had and not allow himself to wish for the impossible. At least he would have their child to love even if he could never have Zoë.

'R&R?'

'Rest and relaxation. Everything has been very intense recently, hasn't it? I think we both need to recharge our batteries.'

'So what do you suggest?' she asked cautiously.

'That we have a day out and get away from it all.'

'It sounds good to me,' she said wistfully. 'Although I'm not sure if I'm up to anything too physically challenging.'

'I realise that, Zoë. But a gentle walk, followed by a pie and a pint at the nearest hostelry wouldn't go amiss, would it?'

'I don't know about the pint, but I could manage an orange juice,' she said tartly, and he laughed.

'Orange juice it is. So how about it? We could make it this Saturday. I've nothing planned, have you?'

'Only flat hunting.' She groaned. 'I'm dreading it. There's nothing worse than trailing round a lot of dreary flats.'

'Then put it off for another week,' he urged. 'You need time to chill out and relax.'

'It is tempting…'

'So it's a date, then? You'll come?' Ben tried not to sound too eager. He wasn't sure why he was so keen to spend the day with her and decided not to worry about it. He grinned when she nodded. 'Great! I'll pick you up on Saturday around ten.'

Zoë agreed that would be fine and he left it there. They chatted about all sorts of things as they completed their journey and he was delighted that everything felt so *normal*. They had always found it easy to talk to one another in the past and if they could get back to that, he would be delighted.

He certainly didn't want them to be arguing all the time. It wasn't good for Zoë or the baby so he resolved to keep things on as even a keel as possible. It didn't alter his decision not to let her back into his heart, of course: nothing would. But if he and Zoë could be friends again, it would be so much better.

He sighed softly. Once upon a time he'd wanted so much more than friendship from her but it hadn't happened. She hadn't been able to love him as much he'd loved her and he'd accepted that. But no matter what happened in the future, he would never love anyone the way he had loved Zoë.

CHAPTER FOURTEEN

SATURDAY dawned bright and clear, the perfect weather for their outing. If Zoë was honest, though, she'd been praying for rain. She would have had an excuse to cancel their trip then. Although it may have seemed like a good idea at the time, she couldn't help wondering if it was a mistake to spend the day with Ben. However, what he had told her in the car had stayed with her. She couldn't stop him getting hurt and if it helped even in a small way to spend this time with her, how could she refuse?

She finished getting dressed, adding a fleece jacket over the top of her trousers and sweater. Her pregnancy was becoming more noticeable so she'd gone into town after work the previous day and bought herself some new trousers, ones with stretchy waistbands that allowed for further expansion. Although some women found it difficult to accept their changing figures, Zoë took comfort from the fact that her baby was thriving despite everything else that was happening.

Ben arrived on the dot of ten, tooting his horn as he drew up outside. Zoë waved to him from her bedroom window then made sure that the scarf was firmly anchored around her head. She'd been touched by the way her colleagues had reacted the first time she'd worn it to work. Abby had hugged her and told her she looked great, and Jason had given her a wolf-whistle.

Zoë smiled as she recalled it. It had been so much better than everyone pretending they hadn't noticed.

Ben had the car door open. He grinned as she slid into the passenger seat. 'Gorgeous day, isn't it? Looks as though the gods are smiling down on us.'

'It certainly does.'

Zoë fastened her seat belt, trying not to notice how handsome he looked, but it was impossible. The rugged clothing he was wearing suited him perfectly. A heavy cream wool sweater over a green-and-brown checked shirt made his shoulders appear broader than ever, while the khaki cargo pants emphasised the muscular length of his legs. He smelled good too, sort of woodsy and masculine, and she sniffed appreciatively before she made herself stop. This wasn't a date. They were having a day out, recharging their batteries. It made no difference how great Ben looked or how good he smelled—they weren't going to end up in bed!

'I thought we'd go to Fell Foot park. I checked their website and apparently the daffodils are still blooming.' He grinned at her. 'We can do a bit of wandering about like two lonely clouds.'

'Ouch!' Zoë winced, glad to change the subject to something less stressful. 'I'm not sure Wordsworth would appreciate you murdering his wonderful poem.'

'I'm not murdering it. I'm paying homage to it.'

She shook her head. 'You could justify any dastardly deed if you set your mind to it.'

'Thank you. I shall take that as a compliment.'

He laughed out loud, making her laugh as well. It was hard not to feel cheerful when Ben was in this mood, she thought. They drove to Fell Foot park on the banks of Lake Windermere and parked the car. Ben reached over into the back seat and handed Zoë a paper carrier bag.

'I bought this for you this morning. It may be sunny today, but it's quite cold outside too. I hope you like it.'

Zoë gasped as she peered into the bag. It was a hat, but not just any old hat. This hat was an absolute riot of colours, red and blue, yellow and purple, orange and green. It was covered in little woolly spikes—like a jester's cap—and each one had either a bell or a tiny mirror sewn onto it. It was a hat to be seen in, one that would attract maximum attention, and she understood immediately why Ben had bought it for her.

'It's lovely. Really lovely. Thank you.'

'I'm glad you like it.'

His voice was so tender that her heart overflowed. Ben was telling her in his own inimitable way that he didn't care if she'd lost her hair, that he didn't care who knew it either. It was hard not to be touched.

Zoë slipped off her scarf and pulled on the hat, leaning sideways so she could see herself in the rear-view mirror. The bells tinkled and the mirrors sparkled, and she laughed in delight. 'It's the nicest present I've ever had!'

'And you are the bravest person I've ever met.'

Ben's voice was filled with so much emotion that she turned to look at him. He was so close that she could see her own reflection in his eyes, tiny images of herself overlaid against the warm hazel colour. It seemed so right, so fitting, to see herself there that she reacted instinctively. Reaching over, she kissed him on the mouth, letting her lips fit themselves to his. His mouth felt so warm, so vital, that she murmured appreciatively. Kissing Ben was like finding herself again after being lost in some dark and scary place. It was like coming home.

'Time for that walk, I think. There's a host of golden daffodils just waiting for us to ooh and ahh over them.'

Ben gently set her from him and opened the car door. Zoë

blinked as a blast of chilly air flowed into the car. For a moment she had difficulty understanding what was happening and then her heart seemed to stutter to a stop. On leaden legs she climbed out of the car, trying to quell the hot rush of sensations that was flooding through her. She couldn't allow herself to feel this way, *mustn't* allow herself to want Ben. It wouldn't be right to use sex to assuage her fears, certainly wouldn't be fair to Ben to play fast and loose with his feelings. It made no difference that she wanted him in every way possible and not just sexually. She couldn't take the comfort and security he could give her and know in her heart that he might suffer because of her selfishness. She loved him too much to do that.

Ben could feel his heart pounding. He could feel his blood pressure soaring too. He could also feel other parts of his body doing things he had sworn they wouldn't do, but, hell's teeth, he was only flesh and blood. And that kiss had pushed him beyond the limit. Did Zoë have any idea how much he wanted her at this moment?

He stamped down hard on that thought as he turned to face her. She looked so beautiful as she stood there with that ridiculous hat on her head that he almost wavered. What he wanted most of all was to sweep her into his arms and carry on where they had left off, only he knew it would be a mistake. Zoë may have instigated that kiss but nothing had changed. She still didn't need *him*.

'Where shall we start?' He forced himself to smile even though his heart had turned to lead at the thought. 'Up here or down by the water?'

'I'm easy. You choose.'

She returned his smile but Ben could see the wariness in her eyes and knew that she regretted what she'd done. He glanced along the path that led to the lake because there was no point making a meal of the fact when it was what he had expected. 'We'll head down towards the water then.'

'Fine.'

Zoë tucked her hands into the pockets of her jacket and set off down the footpath, and Ben's mouth compressed. Did she have to make it so obvious that she didn't want him touching her? They walked in silence for several minutes before she suddenly stopped.

'Oh, look! Over there. It's just glorious.'

Ben turned to look as well. The whole of the bank to their left was a sea of yellow, hundreds of daffodils nodding their golden heads in the sunlight. 'It's beautiful,' he agreed, watching as the breeze made all the flowers dip and bob, creating a wave of yellow that rippled across the banking.

'I don't think I've ever seen so many daffodils!' Zoë exclaimed. She turned shining eyes to him. 'Thank you for bringing me—it's just magical.'

'I'm glad you like it,' he said softly, touched by her delight. It seemed to lighten the mood and restore a measure of harmony so for the next hour they kept up an easy conversation as they wandered along the paths. It was only when Ben realised that Zoë was starting to flag that he called a halt.

He led her back to the car and opened the door. 'How about a spot of lunch? There's a little pub not too far from here that does great food.'

'Sounds good to me.' She slid into the seat with a sigh of contentment. 'I really enjoyed that walk, although I have to admit that I could do with a sit-down now.'

'One sit-down coming right up.' Ben closed the door and hurried round to the driver's side. He cast her a quick glance as he started the engine. 'You haven't overdone it, I hope?'

'Probably. But it was good to do something different for a

change.' She shrugged when he looked at her. 'The trouble with
any illness is that it takes over your life, but I've been able to
forget about it while we've been here and that's been such a treat.'

'I don't know how you cope,' Ben said truthfully. 'I find it
hard to think of anything else—it's constantly on my mind.'

'I'm causing you an awful lot of trouble,' she said sadly.

'I wouldn't have wanted it any other way, Zoë.'

They both fell silent after that. Ben guessed that she was still
worrying about her decision to come back to Dalverston, but
he'd meant what he'd said—he wouldn't have wanted her to
deal with this on her own. He wanted to be here for her.

The pub was busy when they arrived but they managed to
find a table in the corner. It was a typical Lake District pub, un-
changed for years from the look of the old wooden tables and
settles, but that was part of its charm. Zoë smiled as she sat
down and looked around.

'This is great, but how did you find it? It's well off the
beaten track.'

'A patient told me about it. He'd cut his hand on some barbed
wire and while I was sewing him up, we got chatting. He told
me they served the best pint of bitter in the whole of Cumbria
here and he was right. It's worth the drive just to sample it!'

'I'll take your word for it.' Zoë laughed as she picked up a
menu. 'I'll stick to orange juice, thank you.'

They both decided to have the hotpot, a tasty beef and vegetable stew with a light-as-air pie crust. Zoë made rapid inroads
into her meal, sighing as she scooped up the last forkful.

'I haven't enjoyed a meal so much for ages.'

'It must be the fresh air,' Ben observed.

'That, plus the fact that I don't feel sick today. I've had a
couple of days off from my chemo and that has helped, plus
I'm past the feeling sick stage when it comes to the baby.'

'It must be a relief,' he said, thinking what a massive under-statement that was.

'It is. Small mercies, etcetera.'

She smiled at him and Ben felt his throat close up. She was so brave that he was in awe of her resilience. They finished their drinks and headed back to Dalverston. Zoë immediately fell asleep and he didn't wake her. The rest would do her good, help to restore her strength. She didn't wake up until they reached the town centre, looking surprised and a little embarrassed about having slept for so long.

'You should have woken me.'

'What for? You obviously needed the sleep.'

'I did,' she conceded, stifling a yawn. 'What I'd like now to round off the day is a long hot soak in the bath but, sadly, there's no chance of that. There's only a shower in the guests' bathroom at the B&B,' she explained.

Ben slowed the car as they reached a junction and turned to look at her. 'You can have a bath at my place, if you like.'

'Oh, no, I couldn't…really.'

'Why not?' He cut short her protests. 'There's loads of hot water and I'll even throw in some bubble bath as an added in-centive. One of my sisters left it when she stayed with me and it's just sitting in the bathroom cabinet.'

'It's very tempting but are you sure you don't mind? I don't want to put you to any trouble.'

'It's no trouble.'

He pulled out onto the main road and headed towards the apartment before she could come up with any more excuses. If she wanted a bath, a bath was what she would have. It wasn't much to ask, after all. He went straight to the main bathroom after he let them in and turned on the taps then found the bottle of bubble bath.

'Raspberry and passion fruit,' he said, reading the label. 'Sounds more like a cocktail than something you put in the bath water.'

Zoë took it from him and unscrewed the top. 'Hmm, it smells nice, too, good enough to drink, in fact.'

'Don't be tempted,' he warned her with a grin. 'The last thing we need is you foaming at mouth!'

'Definitely not.' Zoë chuckled as she added a generous measure of bubble bath to the water. 'I wouldn't like to have to explain that to Daniel Walker when I see him on Monday morning for my check-up.'

'I doubt he'd be overly impressed,' Ben agreed, reaching up to take some towels off the shelf. 'I think that's everything... Oh, what about a bathrobe? I don't have a spare so I'll lend you mine.'

He fetched it then left her to enjoy her soak. Walking into the kitchen, he switched on the kettle to make himself a cup of coffee then changed his mind when he remembered what she'd said about the smell of coffee making her feel nauseous. He made tea instead and sat in the kitchen to drink it, feeling more relaxed than he'd felt for a while. Ever since Zoë had moved out, he'd been on edge, worrying about how she was coping, and it was a relief to know that she was only in the next room.

His heart skipped a beat as an image of her lying in the scented water appeared in his mind's eye. Her skin would be flushed from the warmth of the water and he groaned as he imagined how it would feel—so smooth and silkily moist. Mentally, Ben let his hands explore her body, following the familiar dips and curves. He knew from that time they'd made love that her breasts were fuller now that she was pregnant and could envisage how they would feel when he held them in his palms. Her waist, too, would no longer be as slender as it used to be, but it didn't dampen his ardour. Their child was growing inside her and he loved the changes her pregnancy had brought about.

He sighed. Nothing would stop him wanting Zoë. Neither time nor distance nor anything else. It was time he faced his feelings instead of avoiding them. He still loved her and he always would. His feelings for her ran too deep; they were part of him as vital to his well-being as breathing and sleeping. He could never tell her how he felt, never risk being rebuffed again, but that made no difference. He loved her and he would be devastated if anything happened to her.

Zoë forced herself to get out of the bath and not before time either. She'd been lying in the water for so long that her fingertips had shrivelled up. She dried herself off then pulled on Ben's robe. It was far too big for her but she rolled up the sleeves and fastened the belt around her waist. The main thing was that it was warm and cosy, and it smelled of Ben.

She sighed as she headed into the bedroom to get dressed. She had missed being here with Ben so much. It was only now that she was back in the apartment that she would admit it. Living here had made her feel safe, something she hadn't felt since she'd moved out. She knew if she told Ben that he would invite her to come back and, although it was tempting, it would be the wrong thing to do. Ben didn't need the pressure of having her living here. He should be able to come home from work and forget about her.

It was a dispiriting thought and seemed to undo all the good the day had done. Zoë felt a wave of exhaustion wash over her and sat down on the bed. It was very quiet in the apartment and it wasn't long before she found her eyes closing. Maybe she should have a nap? Ben wouldn't mind; he'd probably encourage her to take it easy, and that was all the incentive she needed. Curling up on her side, she closed her eyes.

* * *

Ben had heard Zoë go into the bedroom and when she didn't reappear, he couldn't help worrying. What if she'd been taken ill? She might be lying there this very moment, unable to call for help.

He shot to his feet and hurried along the hall. The door was partly open and his heart lurched when he saw her lying on the bed. A couple of strides was all it took to reach her and that was when he realised that she was fast asleep.

His breath huffed out as his panic subsided. He turned to leave then decided that he should cover her up with the quilt. After all, she'd just got out of the bath and he didn't want her catching a chill. Lifting up the edge of the quilt, he tucked it around her, pausing when she opened her eyes.

'I was just covering you up in case you caught a chill.'

'Thank you.' Her voice was husky with sleep and exhaustion, and his heart melted. Sitting down on the edge of the mattress, he took hold of her hand.

'Why don't you stay here tonight? It's obvious that you're worn out and it seems silly to go trailing back to the B&B when there's no need.'

'It's kind of you, Ben, but I don't want to be a nuisance.'

'You could never be that.' He kissed her on the cheek then smiled into her eyes. 'Say you'll stay, Zoë. For my sake. At least when you're here, I know that you're safe.'

Her eyes filled with tears as she clung to his hand. 'It's not fair that you should have to worry about me.'

'Nothing about this situation is fair, Zoë. We just have to deal with it the best way we can.' He drew the quilt around her shoulders and went to get up but she held on to his hand.

'Will you stay with me?' She looked beseechingly up at him. 'I…I feel safer when I'm with you.'

'Of course I'll stay.'

Ben was deeply moved by the admission although he knew it would be wrong to make too much of it. Zoë was fiercely independent and it was merely an indication of how exhausted she must feel to admit such a thing. He lay down beside her and drew her into his arms. She sighed as she snuggled against him.

'This feels nice.'

'Good.'

He brushed the top of her head with a kiss then settled himself against the pillows. Zoë gave another sigh as she relaxed against him, her body fitting itself so snugly against his that he could feel the fullness of her breasts and the swell of her stomach pressing against him. Predictably, his own body made its own pronouncement about how it felt to be in this position but he ignored the rush of desire that swept through him. He wasn't going to do anything to make her feel uncomfortable, certainly wasn't going to let sex intrude. Zoë needed comfort and security and that's what he would give her. In spades!

He lost track of how much time elapsed before he felt her stir. He smiled down at her, pleased to see that she had some colour in her cheeks. 'How do you feel now?'

'Much better. What time is it?'

Ben swivelled his wrist until he could see the dial on his watch. 'Would you believe that it's almost eight o'clock?'

'Eight o'clock? But I must have been asleep for *hours*!'

'Uh-huh.' Ben chuckled. 'You definitely deserve an A-star for sleeping. And as for the snoring…what can I say?'

'I don't snore!'

'How do you know? When you're asleep you have no idea what you do.'

She huffed a bit, unsure whether to take offence, and he grinned at her, clamping down on the desire he felt to kiss her.

It would be inexcusable to take advantage of the situation, no matter how much he longed to do so.

'Ben.'

Her voice was so soft as she whispered his name that for a moment he thought he'd imagined it. However, the expression in her eyes soon set him straight. His heart gave an almighty leap as he looked into her eyes and realised that she wanted him as much as he wanted her. The discovery broke down the restraints he'd placed upon himself. He pulled her back into his arms and this time he knew that neither of them would sleep for a very long time.

CHAPTER FIFTEEN

Dawn was a pale grey streak along the horizon when Zoë awoke the next morning. They hadn't drawn the curtains so she lay in Ben's arms and watched as a new day began, wishing it could be the start of a new life for them. Before she'd met Ben she hadn't believed love existed. It had been a romantic fantasy, a conceit, not something real, live, tangible; something felt by people like her.

Now she knew better. She loved Ben so much and, after last night, she was sure that he cared about her. While the thought filled her with elation, it also filled her with fear. Ben would suffer terribly if anything happened to her and that was the last thing she wanted to happen.

'Penny for them.'

She jumped when he spoke, feeling her heart fill with joy when she turned to look at him. She was the luckiest woman alive to have Ben to take care of her.

'Cheapskate!' she retorted, smiling at him. 'I'll have you know that my thoughts are worth a lot more than a measly penny.'

'Are they indeed? Well, pardon me.' He raised himself up on his elbow and regarded her quizzically. 'So how much are they worth? One pound? Ten?'

'Keep going,' she ordered, enjoying the game when she knew

how it would end. A delicious little shiver rippled through her as she imagined herself back in his arms while they made love again before she forced herself to behave. She was halfway to being a mother and she shouldn't be harbouring thoughts like these!

'Hmm, I'm not sure if I can afford to go much higher. How about if I pay you in kisses instead? Half a dozen per thought for starters, although we can up the fee if you don't think it's enough.'

He leered at her, making her laugh. 'You'd do anything to have your wicked way with me, wouldn't you, Ben Nicholls?'

'Too right I would. Come here!'

He pulled her into his arms and kissed her long and thoroughly so that they were both trembling by the time the kiss ended. Resting his forehead against hers, he let out a groan. 'I really shouldn't have done that. Now I'm going to have to take a cold shower.'

'You don't have to,' she purred, wriggling closer.

'Oh, yes, I do.' He dropped a kiss on her nose. 'I've already kept you awake for half the night and you need your rest. Stay here and I'll make you some breakfast as a penance after I've finished showering.'

Tossing back the quilt, he got out of bed and Zoë gulped when she was presented by the sight of his naked body. Her eyes greedily drank in the glory of the hard muscles under the tanned skin, the long, strong line of his spine and the taut curve of his buttocks. Ben was as beautiful on the outside as he was on the inside, the perfect partner for any woman. How could she have been so blind not to have realised that before? She had forfeited her chance of happiness through her own stubbornness and fear, and it would be wrong to snatch at it now when it could cause him pain. Ben deserved so much more than she could offer him. He deserved a whole lifetime of happiness to look forward to.

Sadness overwhelmed her as she watched him pick up the

robe and pull it on. He turned to her, the first pale streaks of daylight emphasising the masculine perfection of his features. 'What do you fancy? Tea and toast, or the full works—bacon, eggs, sausage, etcetera? I don't know about you, but I'm starving. It must be all the exercise.'

'I could do with a drink,' Zoë murmured. She drummed up a smile, not wanting him to guess there was anything wrong. 'Weak tea preferably.'

'Weak tea it is.'

He headed into the bathroom and a moment later she heard the shower running. As soon as he had finished, she showered too and got dressed. Ben was in the kitchen when she went to find him. He looked up in surprise when he heard her footsteps, his expression changing to consternation when he saw that she was dressed.

'I think it would be best if I went back to the B&B,' Zoë told him before she changed her mind. It would be all too easy to stay when it was what she wanted so desperately, but she couldn't do it. Every extra minute they spent together would make it that much more difficult for him in the future and she couldn't bear the thought.

'At least drink your tea before you go,' he said flatly, pouring tea into a china mug.

Zoë sat down at the table, nodding her thanks when he placed it in front of her. He sat down opposite her, looking grim as he cradled his own cup between his hands.

'What's brought this on, Zoë? I got the impression before that you were quite happy to be here, so what's changed?'

'I've had time to think and realised it's best if I leave. If I stay, it will only make the situation more difficult.'

'Difficult for whom? Not for me, Zoë.'

'Please, Ben, just accept that I know what I'm doing. I don't want to hurt you...'

'And that's why you're leaving, is it? Again?' His voice was filled with scorn and she flushed but she was determined to do what was right.

'Yes. Please try to understand that I'm doing this for your sake as much as my own.'

'Really?' Pushing back his chair, he strode to the window and stood there with his back towards her. There was an ache in his voice that tore at her heart when he continued. 'All I want to do is help you, Zoë.'

'I know that,' she began but he didn't let her finish.

'Do you?' he demanded, swinging round. 'It doesn't appear that way from where I'm standing.'

'I don't suppose it does, but it's true. However, I've come to realise that the more time we spend together, the more difficult it will be for you if anything happens to me.' Her voice was strong because she was sure she was right and his mouth thinned.

'And you think that by pushing me away and refusing my help you're protecting me?'

'Yes. I don't know if the chemo will work, but I do know that my life could end sooner than I expected it would.'

'Nobody knows when their life will end! I could live to be a hundred or I could die tomorrow.' He crossed the room and knelt in front of her. 'I know you can't give me a guarantee that you'll still be here in ten years' time. I can't give you a guarantee like that either. All I can do is promise you that I shall be here for you for the rest of my life if you'll let me, Zoë.'

'Ben, don't...please.' She placed her hand on his cheek, tears welling into her eyes when he turned his head and kissed her palm with such tenderness. He hadn't said that he loved her and she didn't blame him. Why should he open his heart to her again after the last time? The thought of hurting him like that again was more than she could bear and she shook her head.

'I can't accept your offer, Ben. It isn't fair when I have so little to offer you in return. So long as I know that you'll be here for our baby, that's all I ask.'

For a moment she thought he was going to protest, then all of a sudden he rose to his feet. 'If that's how you feel, I have to accept it.'

'Thank you.'

She stood up as well, her legs trembling with the force of the emotions that were bubbling inside her. She could tell that he was hurt by her refusal to accept his help but she had to stick to her decision. At least this way he would be able to protect himself from the worst of the pain.

He picked up his keys. 'I'll run you home.'

Zoë followed him from the room, knowing that there was no going back and no way that she could change her mind. She'd done what she'd had to do, but she wouldn't be surprised if Ben wanted nothing more to do with her after this. The thought filled her with desolation. She couldn't imagine how bleak life would be without Ben.

In the weeks following Zoë's decision, Ben plumbed new depths of despair. His only consolation was that he hadn't told her how much he still loved her. At least he'd spared himself that humiliation and now all he could do was focus on the baby. He intended to be there for his son or daughter, no matter what. Zoë might not need his help but their child did.

In an effort to get back onto an even keel, he threw himself into his work. The department still had a number of vacancies and when Sam took some leave, it meant the department was struggling to cope. Ben went in early most days and stayed on long after he should have finished. His dedication earned him a few pithy comments from the team about him earning extra brownie points, but he laughed them off. So long as nobody knew the real reason why he was so keen to work, he didn't care.

Zoë continued working and receiving her chemotherapy. She was approaching the six-month mark in her pregnancy and Ben knew that she would need to finish work soon, although he didn't ask her if she'd set a date. He treated her as he would any other member of the team, and if it caused him untold heartache, that was his problem.

When she asked him one day if he would like to sit in while she had a scan, he agreed. The least they could be was civil to one another, although the sight of his unborn child on the monitor nearly caused him to reconsider. It was such an emotional occasion, one that both parents should have celebrated as a couple, but he managed to rein in his emotions because it was what Zoë wanted. When they were asked if they wanted to know the sex of their baby, he left it to Zoë to decide and she declined. Whether she preferred it to be a surprise, he wasn't sure and didn't ask. It was her decision.

Another week passed and the staffing situation didn't improve. Although Sam was back at work, Adam had gone off sick. In the end Ben volunteered to work on the Saturday night. The evening started off slowly enough but gradually picked up. By midnight ED was running at full stretch. There were a lot of parties that weekend as teenagers from the local high school celebrated the end of their exams, and more than a few had come to grief thanks to the combination of too much alcohol and high spirits.

Ben was ushering one young girl out of the cubicle after suturing a rather nasty cut on her arm when there was a fracas near the entrance. Two gangs of youths were fighting, overturning chairs and sending people waiting to be seen scattering.

'Phone Security,' he ordered as he hurried over to sort out the melee. Wading into the middle of the group, he raised his voice. 'That's enough! Either you stop now or you'll spend the night in the police cells.'

Most of the boys stopped fighting immediately, but one boy, older than the others, turned on him. 'Who says?'

'I do.' Ben stood his ground. 'If anyone is injured, go over to the desk and register so you can be treated. The rest of you can leave. Now.'

There was a lot of mumbling but the gangs broke up. Two of the boys presented themselves at the reception desk while the others left. Ben took their case notes from the receptionist.

'We'll see this pair straight away. The sooner we get rid of them, the better.'

He ushered the first boy into a cubicle and asked Jason to look after the second. 'OK, so tell me what happened.'

'Someone hit me with a bottle.' The youth turned so that Ben could see the gash running across the back of his scalp. It was bleeding profusely and Ben winced.

'That looks nasty.' He checked the boy's notes. 'OK, Simon, I'm going to have to check that there's no fragments of glass in it. It could sting a bit so grit your teeth, son.'

He used a magnifying glass to examine the cut and discovered that there were several splinters embedded in the boy's scalp. 'Just as I thought—there's glass in it. I'll give you something to ease the pain before I get it out.'

Ben administered a shot of local anaesthetic then, using forceps, managed to extract the glass. Simon looked decidedly green by the time he'd finished and Ben patted him on the shoulder. 'It won't be long now. Just a few stitches and that will be it.' Picking up the needle, he carried on talking, hoping to distract the boy while he got the job done. 'What started this ruckus?'

'One of the other lads said I was chatting up his girlfriend.

We'd gone to a club to celebrate finishing our exams, you see, and that's where it all kicked off. He went absolutely ape, wouldn't listen to a word I said when I tried to explain that all I'd done was apologise for bumping into her. I mean, I wouldn't chat her up even if I was *desperate*. She's a real slapper!'

'I hope you didn't tell him that.' Ben sighed when Simon flushed. 'Not the most diplomatic thing to say, was it?'

'S'ppose not.'

Simon seemed disinclined to say anything else so Ben finished suturing the cut, then ran through the usual instructions about keeping the wound dry and making sure that Simon sought medical help if he felt dizzy or started vomiting. Although it was only a scalp wound, there was a faint chance that the blow could cause Simon mild concussion and Ben wanted to be sure he knew what to do. Jason had finished attending to Simon's friend and the two boys left together, Ben hoping sincerely that they would have the sense to go straight home. To his mind they'd had enough excitement for one evening.

The thought had barely crossed his mind when he heard someone shouting outside the building. It didn't take a genius to work out that the other boys must have been waiting for Simon and his friend to reappear. Ben ran to the exit, his temper spiralling when he saw two boys scuffling on the ground. One was Simon and the other was the older youth who'd confronted him earlier.

'What the hell do you think you're doing?' Ben shouted, grabbing hold of the youth's arm as he went to punch Simon. 'Stop this right now.'

He managed to separate the pair, feeling relieved when a couple of security guards came and took charge. He would leave it to them to decide what to do with the boys. He headed back inside and was just opening the swing door when he heard someone shout and the next moment he felt something punch him hard in his side.

Ben stared in disbelief at the knife that was sticking out of his body. The strange thing was that he didn't feel any pain, just a sort of warmth that seemed to start in the centre of his chest and spread outwards. He crumpled to the floor and his last thought before he slid into unconsciousness was of Zoë. He loved her so much, so very, very much…

Zoë has just turned off her bedside lamp when she heard someone knock on the front door of the B&B. The baby had shifted position during the day and was pressing on her bladder so she'd been up and down to the bathroom umpteen times. Picking up her alarm clock, she peered at the dial. 2 a.m.! Who on earth could be making such a racket at this hour?

She settled down to sleep but she'd only just closed her eyes when someone knocked on her bedroom door. She hastily got out of bed, her eyes widening when she discovered Sam Kearney and her landlady standing outside.

'This gentleman says that you know him, Dr Frost,' her landlady announced, obviously unhappy about being woken at such an hour.

'Yes, I do. Dr Kearney and I work together at the hospital.' She turned to Sam, her heart skipping a beat when she saw how grave he looked. 'What is it, Sam? Why have you come here?'

'I've some bad news for you, Zoë.' Sam took her arm and steered her back into the room. He sat her on the bed and took hold of her hand. 'It's Ben. I'm afraid he's been hurt, badly hurt.'

'Hurt? But how? He was working tonight…' She tailed off, unable to muster her thoughts into any order. Sam squeezed her fingers.

'There was an incident outside ED—a couple of youths

were fighting. Ben went out to break it up and was on his way back into the building when he was stabbed.'

'Stabbed,' she echoed.

'Yes. It's bad too, Zoë. The surgeons are working on him now, but it's touch and go whether he'll make it.' Sam squeezed her hand again, his face filled with compassion. 'I thought you'd want to know.'

'I need to be there. I need to be with Ben, *he* needs me!' She jumped to her feet and felt the room whirl. Taking a deep breath, she forced the dizziness away. 'I'll get dressed. You'll give me a lift to the hospital, won't you?'

'Of course I will. But there's really nothing you can do, Zoë. Ben could be in Theatre for hours…'

'It doesn't matter. I want to be there when he wakes up.'

Zoë could tell from the look on Sam's face that he wasn't sure if Ben would wake up but she didn't dwell on the thought. As soon as Sam left, she dragged on some clothes and grabbed her bag. Her landlady saw her out, murmuring sympathetically that she hoped Dr Frost's friend would be all right.

Zoë hoped so too, but she had no idea what was going to happen, if Ben would survive… A wave of panic gripped her but she refused to fall apart when Ben needed her. She had to be strong for his sake, had to believe that he would pull through. He had to! She couldn't manage without him.

In that second she realised how stupid she'd been these last few months, denying herself precious time she could have spent with him. She'd got it wrong, very wrong. It wasn't the future that mattered but the present. If he survived, she would tell him how sorry she was and that from now on she wouldn't waste another second.

She took a deep breath. She would also tell Ben how much she loved him and needed him…if it wasn't too late.

CHAPTER SIXTEEN

'As YOU can see, the knife entered the body just here.'

Zoë nodded as Jack Devine, Chief of Surgery, pointed to the image that was being displayed on the screen. It was one of a series of X-rays that had been taken before Ben had undergone surgery and if it was anything to go by, she was dreading seeing the rest. They would prove just how serious his injuries were.

'It was a standard kitchen knife with a six-inch blade. It was used with some force because it was buried up to the hilt. Needless to say, it penetrated all the soft tissue in that area.'

Jack Devine's tone was emotionless. Did he have any idea how hard it was to listen to these details when they concerned the man she loved? Zoë wondered. She shot a glance at the consultant's face but it gave nothing away, and maybe that was a good thing. It would have been so much worse if the surgeon had given the impression that this was a hopeless case.

'How badly damaged was his right kidney?' she asked, doing her best to follow the consultant's example.

'You can see from this…' Jack pointed to the next image '…that the knife entered the kidney at a point roughly two-thirds of the way down. Fortunately, it missed the artery but there was extensive bleeding. Apart from blood loss and shock, my biggest concern now is infection. With a penetrating injury such as this, it's a major consideration.'

'There was no damage to the liver?' Zoë asked, hiding her shudder.

'No, but Ben suffered a pneumothorax which was dealt with by the staff in ED before he went to Theatre.' Jack flicked a switch and the screen went dark. 'It would be wrong to raise your hopes, Dr Frost. The next twenty-four hours are critical.'

'I understand. Thank you.'

Zoë went back to the waiting room after the consultant left. There was nobody else there and it was a relief to have the place to herself. She knew that Ben had been given the very best of care. Jack Devine might be a cold fish, but he was a brilliant surgeon—there was nobody better, in fact. Now it was up to Ben himself to fight back.

She sat down, willing the time to pass swiftly. Every extra hour that Ben survived increased his chances, although it was ironic that she wanted the time to fly just when she'd decided to live every second to the full. When a nurse popped her head round the door to tell her that Ben was back from Recovery and she could see him, Zoë leapt to her feet. If she could make him understand that she was there, she was sure it would help.

He was in the bed nearest to the nursing station, always a bad sign as the sickest patients were placed there. Even though Zoë had been in ICU umpteen times in the past, she couldn't help feeling nervous as she approached the bed. All the tubes and machinery, the wires and the bottles were there for one purpose, to keep Ben alive, but it was distressing to see them and to see Ben lying so still in the bed.

'Sit down.' The nurse—Paula, according to her name tag—placed a chair beside the bed and Zoë sat. 'We're keeping him sedated for now to help ease the shock to his system so he won't know you're here, but if it helps you to talk to him, nobody can hear you.'

'Thank you,' Zoë whispered. She leant over the bed after the nurse left, studying the familiar contours of Ben's face. She knew every line as well as she knew the lines on her own face, she marvelled. Even while she'd been pushing him away, her heart had been storing up the details against a rainy day when she might need them. Please, heaven, that day hadn't arrived.

Regret washed over her as she covered his hand with hers. She had wasted so much precious time. Now all she could do was pray that she would be given the chance to make up for it.

Ben knew that his throat was as dry as dust but it hurt when he tried to swallow. He groaned, wondering why he felt so awful. His head was thumping and there was a throbbing ache in his side that felt as though he'd been kicked by a donkey. Had he been riding the donkeys on the beach and fallen off? If so, his mother would give him gyp!

'Ben, can you hear me?'

A female voice penetrated his consciousness and he frowned. It didn't sound like his mum's voice yet it was familiar. He opened his eyes a crack, saw a face, tried to bring it into focus, and gave up. It was just too difficult.

The next time he woke, he felt a little better. Although his throat still hurt, there was a bit of saliva in his mouth. His side wasn't as painful either, or his head. Opening his eyes, he stared at the ceiling, trying to get his bearings. He knew he wasn't in his own bed but he couldn't decide where he was instead. Turning his head, he felt his eyes widen with shock when he saw all the machinery. He was in ICU but what the heck was he doing here?

'Hey, you. Decided to come back to the land of the living, have you?'

The same voice he'd heard before but this time he recognised it immediately. His heart tried to leap right out of his chest when he saw Zoë. She smiled at him, her face lighting up in a way he had longed to see it do and he had to swallow the lump that came to his throat. Was he dreaming again or was this real? Was Zoë really looking at him with her heart in her eyes?

'Zoë,' he croaked like a bullfrog, ruining the tender moment.

'That's me.' She kissed him ever so lightly on the lips and he groaned in disgust. He deserved better than that miserable little effort!

'Did I hurt you?' she said anxiously, pulling back.

'No. Jus…wan…be'er…kiss,' he muttered.

'Oh, I see!' She leant over him again and this time her lips settled more firmly onto his. In fact, they settled there as though they would never leave and Ben sighed in contentment. Forget his headache and his aching side—he could put up with those. He could put up with anything if it meant Zoë was going to keep on kissing him!

She drew back reluctantly. 'I've been so worried, darling. I thought I was going to lose you.'

'What happened?' Ben asked, reaching for her hand and frowning in frustration when he discovered that his own hand was tethered to the bed by all the wires.

'You broke up a fight outside ED and got hurt.' She bit her lip and he could tell that tears were only a blink away. 'You were stabbed, Ben.'

'Ah! That's why my side hurts,' he murmured, hating to see her looking so upset. 'I haven't been kicked by a donkey.'

Zoë gave a gurgle of laughter. 'Trust you to come up with the most unlikely scenario! I mean, how many donkeys do you encounter on an average day?'

'Not that many, but it's always possible that these things can happen.' He looked steadily back at her, hoping he wasn't imagining this too. He didn't think he could bear it if she didn't feel the way he thought she did. 'Anything's possible, Zoë. Anything at all.'

'You're right. It is.'

She kissed him again, her lips clinging to his in a way that made him feel deliriously happy. Either it was all the drugs that had been pumped into his system, or Zoë was demonstrating that she really did love him. His eyes held hers fast when she drew back because he couldn't bear the tension a moment longer.

'Do you love me, Zoë?'

'Of course I do.' She brushed his mouth with her fingertips. 'I've always loved you. I was just too much of a coward to face up to my feelings in the past.'

'And lately?' he asked because he desperately needed to know. 'Why were you so determined to hide them since you came back?'

'Because I thought you no longer loved me.' She smoothed back his hair. 'I wouldn't blame you, either. I hurt you so much when I left you and I shall always regret that. I promised myself that I would never hurt you again and that's why I've kept you at arm's length recently, or tried to.' She smiled at him. 'I did have a few lapses, if you recall.'

Ben recalled them all right—in glorious detail. However, before he could say anything a nurse appeared.

'You're awake, are you? Good.' She turned to Zoë. 'If you wouldn't mind waiting outside, Dr Frost. Mr Devine will want to see him. I'll call you back in once he's finished.'

Ben could barely hide his frustration as Zoë left. Talk about bad timing! It was an effort to respond politely to the nurse's questions as she checked his obs. She smiled as she put the cap back on her pen.

'Don't worry, she'll be back. She's spent the past two days at your bedside so I doubt she's going to do a runner now.'

'Two days!' Ben gulped, no easy feat when his throat was so swollen. 'Is that how long I've been unconscious?'

'Yes. You were very poorly. Mr Devine did a first-rate job on you. You might not be here if it weren't for his skill.'

'I see,' Ben said soberly, realising how lucky he'd been. He could vaguely remember feeling something punch him in the side but the rest was blank.

He closed his eyes after the nurse left, trying to come to terms with the fact that he'd come so close to dying. He wouldn't have known anything about it, but Zoë would. Zoë would have had to deal with the aftermath and the thought of her suffering was far worse than the thought of his demise. All of a sudden he understood why she had taken the stance she had since she'd come back to Dalverston. She had been trying to protect him. She'd cared less about herself than she had about him and it made him feel very humble.

In that second he realised that he needed to tell her how he felt, that he loved her with all his heart. He'd been afraid to do it before but not any more. What scared him now was the thought of *not* telling her. Living out the rest of his life without her didn't bear thinking about.

Ben was moved out of ICU the following day and placed in a side room off Men's Surgical. Zoë popped in several times but each time there was someone else with him. Everyone in the hospital knew Ben so he had a constant stream of visitors.

Whether it was the aftermath of what had happened, Zoë felt exhausted. Although she longed to be with Ben, she needed to go home and rest. Instead of going to the B&B, though, she went to the apartment and slept the clock round, curled up in

Ben's bed. She felt much better the next morning, but she knew that she couldn't keep pushing herself the way she'd been doing. She needed to rest more for the baby's sake and the only way to do that was by giving up work.

There were the usual formalities to complete so she didn't have time to visit Ben before her shift started. Typically, it was one of those days when everything seemed to take twice as long as usual. When lunchtime arrived she still hadn't managed to see Ben and there was no chance of her going then because there'd been an RTA in the town centre.

It was almost four p.m. before she got away. As she hurried to the lift, she could only guess what Ben must be thinking. She smiled as she pressed the button for the third floor. At least she was on her way to see him now and that was the main thing.

Ben had lost count of the number of people who had been to visit him. Although he appreciated their kindness, he couldn't help wishing that he had a few minutes to himself. Zoë had popped in several times the previous day but each time there'd been someone with him and he hadn't had chance to talk to her on his own. The fact that she hadn't been to see him at all that day gave him cold chills. Had he been wrong to think they could finally sort out the mess they'd made of everything?

He was just about to ask one of the nurses to phone the ED when Zoë walked through the door. She smiled at him, such a brilliant smile that his fears evaporated. Opening his arms, he smiled back at her. 'Come on, then. What are you waiting for? I thought you'd deserted me in my hour of need.'

'Hour of need?' Zoë chuckled as she sat on the bed and let him enfold her in a hug. 'There's been that many people here to minister to your every need, you're in danger of being spoiled!'

'Ah, but they weren't you. And *that* makes all the difference.'

He kissed her hungrily, glorying in the fact that she kissed him back just as eagerly. They both sighed when they drew apart and Ben laughed.

'We needed that, didn't we?'

'I definitely did.' She smoothed his cheek with a gentle hand. 'I love you, Ben Nicholls. Did I tell you that before I went AWOL?'

'I'm not sure.' He pretended to consider the question. 'You did mention something along those lines, but I was a little hazy from all the drugs. Maybe you should tell me again. And again. And again…'

She pressed her fingers to his mouth, effectively silencing him. 'I love you. I made a big mistake by pushing you away and I intend to make up for it, if you'll let me.'

'I understand why you did it, Zoë. You were trying to protect me and I'll always cherish that thought.' He kissed her hand. 'I understood why you've behaved the way you've done when I realised how close I'd come to dying.' His voice caught. 'The thought of your suffering was more than I could bear.'

'Don't! I can't bear to think of anything happening to you, my darling. It's harder for those left behind. They have to deal with their grief as well as the loss of the one they loved. But you're getting better, Ben, and I give thanks for that.'

'And you are, too.' He captured her hands. 'Your treatment is going to work, Zoë. I know it will.'

'I feel really hopeful, too.' She placed his hand on her stomach, seeing his delight when the baby moved. 'This little one is going to grow up with both a mummy and a daddy to love him or her.'

'Zoë!' Words eluded him so Ben settled for the next best thing, or maybe the *very* best thing: a kiss.

Zoë sighed blissfully as she snuggled against him. 'I'm sure we shouldn't be doing this. You've had major surgery and you need to be careful.'

'It's the best medicine in the world, not to mention the biggest incentive to make a speedy recovery.' Ben kissed her again. 'I love you too, Zoë. I tried not to love you but I failed miserably. I gave you my heart two years ago and it's been yours ever since.'

'Oh, Ben, I wish—'

'No.' He kissed her softly on the lips. 'No regrets. It's the future that matters now, not the past.'

'That's exactly how I feel.' She kissed him again, only drawing back when she felt him wince as the stitches in his side tweaked painfully. She stood up, shaking her head when he protested. 'There'll be plenty of time for all that when you're better.'

'Is that a promise?'

'Yes, if you want it to be.'

'You know I do.' Ben looked up at her. 'I want a lot more than that, too, Zoë.'

'Then why don't you tell me what you want?' she said softly.

'You. Will you marry me? Will you live with me for ever and ever and let me love you? Will you make me the happiest and proudest man in the world?'

'Yes, I will.'

She smiled at him, her face alight with love, and Ben's heart swelled with happiness. Raising her hand to his lips, he kissed her palm then closed her fingers over the spot where his mouth had touched. 'Sealed with a kiss, my love. You can't go back on your promise now.'

Zoë leant over and kissed him. 'I shall never go back on it, Ben. You and I are going to spend the rest of our lives together.'

One year later

'Ladies and gentlemen, please be upstanding while we toast the bride and groom.'

Zoë looked at Ben and smiled. They had just been married in a civil ceremony held in the garden of a hotel on the banks of Lake Windermere. All their friends and Ben's family had been invited and she could see the delight on their faces as they stood up for the toast. Heather and her husband Archie were there, too, looking blissfully happy, and Ross and Gemma, who appeared equally thrilled with life. It was obvious that both couples were very much in love.

Ross was acting as Ben's best man and now he held his glass aloft.

'To the bride and groom. May they have many happy years ahead of them.'

Zoë's heart brimmed with happiness as she looked at all the smiling faces before her gaze moved back to the two people she loved most of all. Ben was holding their daughter and once again she was struck by the resemblance between them. At almost nine months old, little Serena Katherine Nicholls was the image of her adoring father, with her dark curls and huge hazel eyes. Zoë knew that she would never get over the wonder of giving birth to this perfect little human being.

Thankfully, her chemotherapy hadn't harmed the baby in any way and Serena had been given a clean bill of health, much to their delight. The fact that Zoë had also been told the previous week that there was no sign of her cancer returning was another reason to celebrate. She had the best incentive in the world to look forward to the future now—a gorgeous baby daughter and an equally gorgeous husband.

'I love you,' she whispered, leaning over so that only Ben could hear her.

'I love you, too.' Ben kissed her hungrily then grinned when a cheer erupted. He dropped a kiss on the baby's head, handed her to Zoë and stood up.

'I just want to thank you all for sharing our very special day. I don't think I need to tell you how much today means to me. I feel like the luckiest man in the world to have such a gorgeous wife and daughter.'

He helped Zoë to her feet. Raising his glass, he turned to face her. 'To my beautiful bride and my equally beautiful daughter. Thank you both for making me so happy.'

Zoë laughed as everyone applauded. It was a moment to treasure, and the best thing of all was that she knew there would be many more times like this to come. She, Ben and Serena had a lifetime of happiness ahead of them.

0309/03a

MILLS & BOON

MEDICAL

On sale 3rd April 2009

A FAMILY FOR HIS TINY TWINS
by Josie Metcalfe

Gorgeous A&E doctor Gideon is deeply protective of his
premature newborn twins. And having lost a baby of her own,
nurse Nadia is devoted to her tiny patients. Nadia's fallen hard
for Gideon and his babies – she'd make a wonderful wife and
mother, if only she could open her heart to him too…

ONE NIGHT WITH HER BOSS
by Alison Roberts

Tama James is outraged to discover that the new member of
his paramedic team is his boss's daughter. But Mikayla Elliot
is everything Tama thought she wouldn't be. Tama is now
determined to show her that he wants her on his
team…and in his bed!

TOP-NOTCH DOC, OUTBACK BRIDE
by Melanie Milburne

When GP Kellie Thorne arrives in the Outback she's
unprepared for her sizzling attraction to brooding colleague
Matt McNaught! But her stay is temporary. To keep her,
Matt must make this Outback doctor his wife.

Available at WHSmith, Tesco, ASDA, and all good bookshops
www.millsandboon.co.uk

0309/03b

MILLS & BOON
MEDICAL*
On sale 3rd April 2009

A BABY FOR THE VILLAGE DOCTOR
by Abigail Gordon

GP Georgina retreated to the idyllic haven of Willowmere
after her marriage broke down. Now her ex-husband Ben
Allardyce has found her – and is stunned to discover that
Georgina is pregnant with their child! Loving her still, he's
determined to make Georgina his bride – all over again…

THE MIDWIFE AND THE SINGLE DAD
by Gill Sanderson

Midwife Alice Muir has returned home to forget her dreams
of having a family, but her new colleague is her childhood
sweetheart Dr Ben Cavendish! Will Ben manage to overcome
his fears and make all Alice's dreams come true?

THE PLAYBOY FIREFIGHTER'S PROPOSAL
by Emily Forbes

Scarred from a childhood heart transplant, Dr Sarah Richardson
has never thought of herself as beautiful and has lived for
her work. Playboy Ned knows he wants more than just
a fling with Sarah. But first he must convince her that
she is perfect – inside and out!

Available at WHSmith, Tesco, ASDA, and all good bookshops
www.millsandboon.co.uk

From governess to mother and wife!

Two brand-new heartwarming historical
romances featuring:

More Than a Governess by Sarah Mallory
The Angel and the Outlaw by Kathryn Albright

**The special gift of a mother's love.
Perfect reading for Mother's Day!**

Available 6th March 2009

www.millsandboon.co.uk

M&B

A Secret Child...
An Irresistible Attraction...
A Passionate Proposition!

THE *Secret*
BABY BARGAIN

BARBARA HANNAY
MEREDITH WEBBER
& MARY NICHOLS

Three brand-new stories featuring:

The Billionaire's Baby Surprise by Barbara Hannay
Expecting His Child by Meredith Webber
Claiming the Ashbrooke Heir by Mary Nichols

Perfect for Mother's Day!

Available 20th February 2009

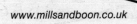

www.millsandboon.co.uk

M&B

Passion. Power. Suspense.
It's time to fall under the spell of Nora Roberts.

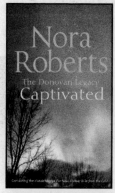

2nd January 2009

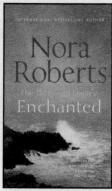

6th February 2009

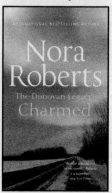

6th March 2009

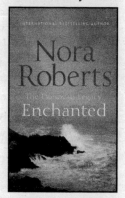

3rd April 2009

The Donovan Legacy

Four cousins. Four stories. One terrifying secret.

309/010/MB207

He's her boss in the boardroom – and in the bedroom!

Her Mediterranean Boss
Three fiery Latin bosses
Three perfect assistants
Available 20th February 2009

Her Billionaire Boss
Three ruthless billionaire bosses
Three perfect assistants
Available 20th March 2009

Her Outback Boss
Three sexy Australian bosses
Three perfect assistants
Available 17th April 2009

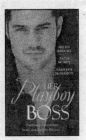

Her Playboy Boss
Three gorgeous playboy bosses
Three perfect assistants
Available 15th May 2009

Collect all four!

www.millsandboon.co.uk

FREE!

4 Books
and a surprise gift!

We would like to take this opportunity to thank you for reading this Mills & Boon® book by offering you the chance to take FOUR more specially selected titles from the Medical™ series absolutely FREE! We're also making this offer to introduce you to the benefits of the Mills & Boon® Book Club™—

- ★ **FREE home delivery**
- ★ **FREE gifts and competitions**
- ★ **FREE monthly Newsletter**
- ★ **Exclusive Mills & Boon Book Club offers**
- ★ **Books available before they're in the shops**

Accepting these FREE books and gift places you under no obligation to buy, you may cancel at any time, even after receiving your free shipment. Simply complete your details below and return the entire page to the address below. You don't even need a stamp!

YES! Please send me 4 free Medical books and a surprise gift. I understand that unless you hear from me, I will receive 6 superb new titles every month for just £2.99 each, postage and packing free. I am under no obligation to purchase any books and may cancel my subscription at any time. The free books and gift will be mine to keep in any case.

M9ZEF

Ms/Mrs/Miss/Mr ....Initials..........................
BLOCK CAPITALS PLEASE
Surname ....
Address...

....Postcode ....

Send this whole page to:
UK: FREEPOST CN81, Croydon, CR9 3WZ

Offer valid in UK only and is not available to current Mills & Boon Book Club subscribers to this series. Overseas and Eire please write for details. We reserve the right to refuse an application and applicants must be aged 18 years or over. Only one application per household. Terms and prices subject to change without notice. Offer expires 31st May 2009. As a result of this application, you may receive offers from Harlequin Mills & Boon and other carefully selected companies. If you would prefer not to share in this opportunity please write to The Data Manager, PO Box 676, Richmond, TW9 1WU.

Mills & Boon® is a registered trademark owned by Harlequin Mills & Boon Limited.
Medical™ is being used as a trademark. The Mills & Boon® Book Club™ is being used as a trademark.